PENGUIN BOOKS

YELLOW IS THE COLOUR OF LONGING

K.R. Meera, an independent journalist and writer, made her mark in Malayalam journalism when she won the PUCL Human Rights National Award for Journalism in 1998 for an investigative series on the plight of women labourers in Kerala. She started writing fiction in 2001 and her first short story collection *Ormayude Njarambu* was published in 2002. Since then she has published four collections of short stories, a novella and three novels. Meera is one of the most widely read authors of her generation in Malayalam and has won many prestigious literary prizes.

J. Devika writes in both Malayalam and English. Her publications include *En-gendering Individuals: The Language of Re-form in Early Modern Keralam* and *Individuals, Householders, Citizens: Malayalees and Family Planning*, and the English translation of the autobiography of Nalini Jameela, *The Autobiography of a Sex Worker*. She is at the Centre for Development Studies, Thiruvananthapuram.

Yellow Is the Colour of Longing

K.R. Meera

Translated from the Malayalam by J. Devika

PENGUIN BOOKS

PENGUIN BOOKS

Published by the Penguin Group

Penguin Books India Pvt. Ltd, 11 Community Centre, Panchsheel Park, New Delhi 110 017, India

Penguin Group (USA) Inc., 375 Hudson Street, New York, New York 10014, USA

Penguin Group (Canada), 90 Eglinton Avenue East, Suite 700, Toronto, Ontario, M4P 2Y3, Canada (a division of Pearson Penguin Canada Inc.)

Penguin Books Ltd, 80 Strand, London WC2R 0RL, England

Penguin Ireland, 25 St Stephen's Green, Dublin 2, Ireland (a division of Penguin Books Ltd)

Penguin Group (Australia), 250 Camberwell Road, Camberwell, Victoria 3124, Australia (a division of Pearson Australia Group Pty Ltd)

Penguin Group (NZ), 67 Apollo Drive, Rosedale, Auckland 0632, New Zealand

Penguin Group (South Africa) (Pty) Ltd, 24 Sturdee Avenue, Rosebank, Johannesburg 2196, South Africa

Penguin Books Ltd, Registered Offices: 80 Strand, London WC2R 0RL, England

The stories in this collection have been selected and translated from the Malayalam collections of K.R. Meera: *Ormayude Njarambu* (Thrissur: Current Books, 2002), *Mohamannjha* (Kottayam: D.C. Books, 2004) and *Ave Maria* (Thrissur: Current, 2006). 'Coming Out' was published in *Malayalam Vaarika* (July 2007) and 'Guillotine' in *Mathrubhumi Weekly* (October 2008). These stories appeared subsequently in her collection *Guillotine* (Thrissur: Current Books, 2010). An earlier version of the translation 'Yellow Is the Colour of Longing' was first published in *Feminist Review* 83 (2008).

First published by Penguin Books India 2011

ISBN 9780143068471

Typeset in Adobe Garamond by InoSoft Systems, Noida
Printed at Chaman Offset Printers, Delhi

Contents

Yellow Is the Colour of Longing

She had jaundice. Really. So everything looked yellow to her. The streaks of grey in his hair, his intelligent eyes, his well-clipped, clean nails, everything. And he—he had a new strain of viral fever. So her curly hair, pale cheeks and the tiny black bindi on her forehead were all grey to him. Sitting in that room in the lodge in Gandhi Nagar, she actually thought that he was a yellow man; he thought she was a grey woman. Poor things. Nothing more than a woman and a man at that moment. She was thirty-five, plus or minus. He, forty-five, plus or minus. She, a divorcee and the mother of two. He, married, the father of two.

Admitted or not, it was sexual interest, commonly found among women and men, that led them into that room in that middling sort of lodge in that suburb of Kottayam. They had infected each other at the Kottayam Medical College. Who is not infected by lust in hospitals? The longings that are liberated from the many thousand bodies of the dead, are they not flitting about in the air there? Like the way the mouldy growth breaks out, its pleasure bristling upon loaves of stale bread, just the way white mushroom-penises sprout, erect, on fallen leaves during the rains, desires burgeon at each faint favourable moment. These were people not loved enough. And sick, besides. Stricken with many different sorts of aborted desire, the body would turn red-hot and then be dispersed into the air as vapour. If only someone intimate with the wizardry of love would utter a magic spell to draw that vapour back inside, making it solid flesh and bones once again—who cannot help wishing for that? One wouldn't bother about tobacco stains on lips, or bad breath, that moment. That's all there is to human beings.

The Communicable Diseases Ward where they met was the twenty-fourth ward of the medical college hospital. It had glass doors, unlike the other wards, with the number twenty-four on them, painted inside a red circle. And again, unlike the other wards, the outpatient section was attached to it. Linked red plastic chairs lay beneath the black-lettered signboard that read 'Dr Sujith Kumar'. That this ward is right next to the gate is most convenient. Even the mortuary is just next door, if the need arises. No wonder we are all made into patients with infectious diseases at the slightest pretext.

She was the first to arrive that day. Rain fell outside, light and frail. He had run in from the rain. Shaking off drops of water from his shirtsleeves and lightly greying hair, he sat in the plastic chair opposite hers. He lifted his head and before anything else, looked directly into her eyes. The way it happens when one falls in love, even though one is setting one's eyes on the other for the first time. Both of them thought: I've seen him somewhere before; I've met her sometime before. Sitting opposite each other, their glances met, greeted each other and parted several times, for no particular reason. Once his glance tripped in her eyes, apologized, got up and left. Another time, her glance stumbled in his, but his eyelashes held her before she fell. In between, when another patient bickered with an attender, he joked and shared a laugh with a neighbour. For some reason he held out to her a slice of that laughter. Then a little later when the woman sitting next to her looked at the OP card and said something, she had to laugh for politeness's sake. That moment she repaid the loan of laughter, the

5

exact amount, he had given her earlier. In between she remembered someone else. As that memory ended, letting go the usual sigh, she raised her eyes, to see him sitting in the chair beside her. He too was in deep thought. She did muse about what might be on his mind. Was he thinking of illness? Of death? Or about his children and wife who would be orphaned if he died? Suddenly she remembered that in the morning's hurry to send the children off to school, she had forgotten her tea. It was that very moment that he turned his head and spoke to her the first time: 'Care for a cup of tea?'

She started. Her reply was slow to come. Just that she reddened a bit.

'Our numbers won't be called so soon ...' he continued.

She felt somewhat embarrassed. Was the desire for tea so sharply etched on her face? The thought made her redden further. Well, whatever that was, she looked at a man with approval after a very long time and gave him a pleased smile.

'Let's go.'

As they walked along the wet footpath, though it wasn't particularly relevant at that moment, she noticed that this was the first time she was walking with a man after the break-up with her husband. Was he worthy of such high honour, she wondered. He was a tall man. His footsteps were firm. But it seemed to her that he was dispirited in his heart of hearts. Women's dissatisfactions show up below their eyes. Men's appear in their stride. She had dark circles beneath her eyes. The intermittent illness that always came back after all the different sorts of treatment disheartened her. She had enough of swallowing medicines and getting blood and urine reports. Today, as she was draping her sari and getting ready for the trip to the hospital, she had even decided that if this doctor too failed to diagnose the illness, she would give up treatment altogether. It was then that her older son came into the room looking for his inhaler. Seeing his little chest struggle for breath, she reversed her decision. Who else would massage his bony back as he gasped for breath, sleepless, through the night, if she wasn't alive? She was all they had. She alone was there to mediate when the kids fought, she alone stayed to attend the PTA meetings at their school, she alone was left to buy them new clothes for Onam, she alone remained to remember their birthdays and get them packets of birthday toffees to take to the school. She alone was there to make the little smiles bloom on their faces.

And then he spoke again: 'Where do you live?'

'At Pandalam.'

'Did you run there from the troops?'* He threw her a mischievous look.

'No, ran there to light the torches!' she replied rather gloomily, thinking all the while of her son. It was when he stared at her, startled, that she realized what she had said and to whom. Who is she? Or, what is she? A woman past thirty-five. Her middle was like a freshly swept front yard, all marked with lines like the streaks the broom leaves behind. Her breasts had lost their self-confidence. Her backside wasn't shapely. And her hair was falling strand by strand, like casuarina leaves flying off with every breeze in winter. Which man would fancy such a woman trying to joke? In short, these days, it is terrible for women past a certain age.

They were inside the coffee house by then. He found by himself a place less afflicted by the generator's awful droning.

'I have seen you somewhere.'

'I work at the LIC.'

'Ah! Good!' He smiled.

'What do you do?'

---

* The reference is to a popular saying in Malayalam which goes 'I ran to Pandalam fearing the army; but there was the army lying in wait, their torches all lit.'

'I'm a teacher. What's your illness?'

'Don't know …' her tone was a disheartened one.

He smiled. 'Lucky lady …'

'What's your sickness?' she inquired.

'Some sort of viral fever. It's almost gone. But I have to get it checked every once in a while.'

The waiter came up with two cups of tea. They drank it in silence. It was he who paid the bill. They were silent until they reached the ward. Her number was called first. She hurried in and described to the doctor some of her symptoms. This doctor too wanted blood and urine reports. She came out, and he went in. Glancing at him as if to say goodbye, she felt a certain perturbation spread to her from him. How many are the different sorts of ailments in this world! Some spread through touch, some through glances. Some through the wind and through messages, letters. Hope Dr Sujith Kumar has remedies for all these.

The lab was crowded. As she stood at the rear of the long queue, he hurried in, looking around as if trying to locate someone in haste. She was amused to see that peculiar demeanour. Who would not be amused to see a man who has greyed a bit, lost some hair, and with a face wrinkled with the burden of worldly cares, look around with adolescence peeping out of his eyes? But when she realized that his adolescence was actually seeking her, her face paled and then reddened; then his eyes sought her out, and he rejoiced at finding her. Her heart filled to the brim. For most women, it is like that. When after many years, a woman is sought out by a man's eyes, and when she is sure that they were indeed seeking her and her alone, she will find her heart brimming. That is of course one good thing about women.

Gently, he came to her. In his case too the doctor had asked for several investigations, he told her. There was a blood test to be done. The result would be ready only by two o'clock. He was planning to meet the doctor with it at the evening's OP. Otherwise he would have to come on Wednesday. She told him that she had decided to come another day to meet the doctor. His face fell when he heard that.

'Why bother with another journey?' he asked. 'Wouldn't it be better to meet the doctor today itself?'

His wrinkled face of forty-five years reddened and paled at once. He struggled not to look at her. Maybe he was scared that his eyes may stick to her body parts and then she would take him to be a lecher. That's the problem with men. They can see women only as bodies. They keep worrying how this woman would judge them in bed. In short, it's terrible for men too, after a certain age.

After the test it seemed as though the evening's OP was a long way off. And then, as if trying to crack a joke, mustering up the courage somehow, he suggested: 'We could have gone for a movie if we were younger.'

She smiled. A moment's silence, and then she asked bravely, 'Which theatre has a show this afternoon?'

Before she finished, they saw a poster right in front. *Kaathal Konden*. Noon show. Why not see that film, he asked. She agreed. They found the theatre, bought the tickets, got in and settled in adjacent seats. The show had already begun. But they could soon follow the story. It was a Tamil film. But they could still make out the dialogues. There weren't many people in the theatre. After the intermission, he gently put his arm on her shoulder. She pretended as if she didn't know. After some time, she mildly rested her head on his shoulder. He too pretended as if he didn't know.

The movie was over by two-thirty. They had lunch at a nearby hotel. There was a lot more time to kill. Somehow then her head began to spin; she sweated profusely and her eyes rolled back; all around her everything looked yellow. He was alarmed. Was she feverish? He checked her forehead and neck with the back of his palm. It was he who decided that the cure for this was to rest awhile somewhere. She too thought it a good idea. And that is how, it so seems, they checked into a nearby lodge.

11

She lay on the white sheets. He sat beside her, caressing her palm. They could see themselves in the mirror just opposite. Two poor souls. People with little time left for love. People too shy to love. Who were too afraid to love. And yet, without the courage to abandon love. She could not take her eyes off his hands. Light-yellow-coloured hands which looked as if they had never even once touched dirt. The nails weren't smudged, like those on the hands she had seen before. They didn't have the yellowish cigarette scar. The palms weren't rough. She looked at her own hands. They were rough, from washing dishes and clothes. The dirt-lined nails had dark borders. What were his wife's nails like? Like hers? He was then thinking of her former husband. Who had given up whom? He, her, or she, him? Wasn't he handsome? Didn't he know how to kiss and cuddle her properly? Who knows women's ways? Some don't like to be kissed. Some can never have enough of it.

He ran his fingers gently down her cheeks. She clasped his hands firmly.

'The yellow, is it gone?'

His tone faltered. 'No ...'

She laughed. 'And you?'

'I still have the fever, right? My eyes are red in one corner, black in the other. Still the same old grey.'

He too laughed. Well, one knows too well what all may happen when a man and a woman have a room to themselves and begin to laugh together. They could well laugh until they cried. Laughing is a kind of magic. When she laughed he felt that she was really good-looking; and when he laughed she thought that he was really good-looking. He felt like kissing her; she felt like kissing him. Needless to say more, these two patients with communicable diseases, these two who had met just that morning, they forgot their homes and their haunts, society and its norms, and, to tell the truth, mated, made love. Waking up later, he kissed her wistfully, and she took it the best she could.

When they checked out, the OP at the medical college had closed. The OP of the stars had opened above. Reaching home, she became worse.

Seeing her lying on the bed, terribly weak, her arm pressed on her forehead, her younger child asked, distressed: 'What's wrong, Mother? Are you feeling too sick?'

'Nothing, Son,' she said haltingly. 'Everything looks a bit yellow—that's all.'

That night she became seriously ill. The children were scared. They woke up the neighbours, who got her to the hospital at once. Her illness was confirmed to be jaundice. They treated her for almost two weeks. In the daze induced by the medicines and the sick diet, she saw him again and again. How funny, she saw him all yellow, even in stupor. Yellow eyes, yellow hair, yellow ears, yellow lips ...

It was nearly a week or so later. The illness cured, she was cleaning up the room, and then she saw him once more, in a scrap of newspaper lying among the plants. Below some writing that mentioned that another teacher had died of jaundice or something like that, all yellow, yellow, yellow ...

Ave Maria

The day PG forswore EM.* Rage welled up again inside Immanuel. Storm clouds piled heavy as he got off the bus at Moscow Junction. Thunder rumbled beneath his footsteps as he strode towards Chorakkod, the house. Jumping over the fence, a flash of lightning, he climbed on to the veranda's mud floor. 'Thieving whore!' he roared. Sixty-five-year-old Anna ran to the neighbour's. Sixty-four-year-old Mary hid beneath the cot, muttering

---

* Reference to leading communists in Kerala—P. Govinda Pillai and E.M. Sankaran Nambudiripad.

terrified prayers. On her coir cot, poor paralytic fifty-nine-year-old Lourdes wet herself again. Immanuel's varicose legs furiously kicked open the door, already reduced to mere planks by kicks and more kicks of the past. Inside, as his weak, long-sighted eyes searched in the dark, Immanuel bellowed, 'DIRTY WHORE! Come out, Mariakutty, comrade Mariakutty, soviet Mariakutty, socialist Mariakutty, republic Mariakutty, chinese Mariakutty, YOU WON'T SEE ANOTHER SUNRISE! I'LL CUT OFF YOUR HEAD! PULP YOUR WOMB! GULP YOUR BLOOD! WASH THIS HOUSE WITH IT! MAKE A COMMIE RED GARLAND OUT OF YOUR BLOODY GUTS! THEN SURRENDER TO THE POLICE. THE POLICE ARE PEANUTS, YOU BITCH!

Immanuel can't see in the dark. Mariakutty lay quiet, pressing herself to the ground. Immanuel's cracked feet would search the floor. Bursting with anger, they would hit against each wall. They would kick at every corner. Sometimes at Anna's torn mat, folded up. Sometimes at Marykutty's bundle. Or at a dried-up coconut found somewhere, fallen off a tree. Or a piece of yam, begged off the neighbours. In between these Mariakutty would lie curled up like an iron sickle. Immanuel would not make out fast. He would kick everywhere. Crush and bruise anything that resisted. Keep on spewing curses.

And then, sometimes, she would be found. Hauled up on a single arm. Just about ten kilos. Nine kilos of bones. The meat, just a kilo. Skin. Eighty-nine years. They are all like that. Age goes up, weight goes down. When bones age, the flesh hangs. Immanuel would toss them around, playing the cat's game with the mouse. Crush them. Grind them to the ground. Kicking, hitting, throwing, Immanuel would tire. His mundu would loosen halfway down. His shirt would be soaked, sweaty. Sweat drops would roll on his bald head, like on a lotus leaf. Eyes would redden and half close. About to collapse, he would stop. Get out. Go the way he came, head bowed. Anna would come back from her running away. Mary would chant aloud, Praise the Lord, Praise the Lord. Lourdes, relieved, would wet herself again.

At night, Immanuel would return, like a lame dog. Anna and Mary and Lourdes would have slept. He would sit on the soiled armchair on the veranda. In his tired voice, he would call, 'Mother …' Pull out the rum bottle from his mundu. Pour out the liquor into a clean or not-so-clean glass kept underneath the armchair. Sit there without sipping, staring into the darkness. Mariakutty would then slowly raise herself up, along the wall. Come out carefully, measuring the floor with her weak eyes. A bit of lime pickle in her broken-edged tin plate. Or a washed green chilly. Sliding the plate close to Immanuel's feet, Mariakutty would sit on the floor, leaning against the wall, silent. Immanuel would take in his drink slowly. Suck at the pickle, in between. Stare at the dark, thinking of the concrete houses sprouting up in the fields, or of the battery factory where the communist paccha weeds thrived. Drink a bit. Think a bit. Drinking, thinking, drinking, thinking, he would fall asleep. Legs would be raised up on the chair. They would curl up when the sleep thickened. He would curl into a 'C', like a tiny baby in its cradle. Suck his thumb in slumber deep. Sob in his dreams. Shake with laughter. Then Mariakutty would stretch her bones and get up. Cover him with her cloth. Wipe the spittle oozing on his greyed beard. Close the open liquor bottles, straighten up the fallen-down ones, push them behind the chair. Creep back inside with the curry plate. Get herself down on the floor with effort. It is then that heavy tears condense. 'Ingila Sindaba ...'* she would chant in a shattered voice.

That's an old habit. Something that Cholakkot Varkey taught her. Varkey, the son of a Varkey, who was the son of an earlier Varkey, of Cholakkot. Known those days as Cholakkodan. Until Putuppally and Toppilaan**

---

* 'Inquilab Zindabad', of course: 'Victory to the Revolution'.
** Two prominent leaders of the communist movement in Kerala of the 1940s.

got to him. Chorakkodan, afterwards. Born rebel. He saw Mariakutty, whose parents had died, now bullied by her sisters-in-law. Got her a new blouse stitched out of heavy-white mulmul. Took her to church to marry. Taught her to cook chilly-and-tapioca. To fry beef with pepper. To reap. To winnow. To be tickled, and to laugh. To play at tiffs and to fret. To give birth to chubby little ones every year. Anna, Mary, Magdalene, Maria ... when Lourdes was in her womb, Putupally, Toppilaan and Potty Sir started appearing. Bidi lights glowed among the tapioca. The kerosene lamp Maria lit began to hear controlled whispers. Anna's slate began to know the shape of the sickle. Baby Maggie began to lisp, Ingila Sindaba. He brimmed over when asked about the meaning of it. Mariakutty, golden one, hot-sweet love, my own wine glass, my daily bread, holy mother. That is a novena. A novena to recite, to call upon. Call upon? Who? Call upon good times. A good time. A time when no one will be sad. Be warned, the police's blows will come—yes, some will come; be warned, the jail—yes, that'll happen; and what about the kids and me? That's what I'm sad about. Why sad? I can also take a few blows. Hey Mariye, you silly, these are police blows. Oh, big deal, I've had five or six kids! But, Mariye, still ... Oh, if no one will go hungry, what's the big deal in suffering a few blows?

So you bred like swine, didn't you? Immanuel spat out
as he delivered another kick. You put together wizened
old crones, not worth five rupees, didn't you? Why?
Couldn't you kill them? Cut them piece them and fry
them in pepper? No, I'll do it myself, I'll kill these swine
myself. He ran after his sisters. The kidney patient, Anna.
Her swollen body. She would run, and she would fall.
The tattered nightgown, the neighbour's gift, would tear.
She would scream aloud. The mental patient, Mary. She
would tug hard at her grey hair. He cometh to deliver
the sinners, she would yell. Lourdes would wet herself
in fear. The son's roaring. The daughters' screaming.
Mariakutty shut her eyes tight. Eyes grown rheumy of
seeing, seeing. Eyes rusted from crying, crying. They
are all like that. The rust to iron. The termite to wood.
They would crumble, speck by speck. Break off, inch by
inch. The night the policemen bit the dust at Sooranad.
The beginning of the flight. Five tiny kids. Three small
bundles. A babe in the left arm, still at the breast. A
toddler in the right. Children, left and right. Don't cry.
Don't play. Don't laugh. Don't make a sound. Don't say
Mama's and Papa's name. Walk. Walk fast. I'm hungry,
Mother. A little water, Mama. Anna wants to lie down.
Mary wants to be picked up. Maria wants beddie-bed.
The January sun beat down. The children wilt. Fall. First,
Adoor. From there, Kottarakkara. Be careful. There's a

reward on Chorakkadan's head. A thousand rupees. A cool thousand. The never-fully-counted one thousand of those days. The heart beats hard, seeing someone on the way. If he looked again, the knees knock. Walk, walk, and finally a house at Valakam. Cooked gruel under the coconut tree. Laid out the mat on the step of the cowshed. The children slept like logs. The eyes then shut, with ears open, and heard muffled sobs. Mariakutty, my jar of wine, sweet grapes … let's go—the kids are sleeping, let them. Take only the infant. What are you saying? —No other way. They are my mark. Five children—oh, my womb burns—Mariye, call out, Ingila Sindaba—my heart will smoulder—Ingila Sindaba —our Annakutty. Marykutty, little Maggie, Maria-baby … —Mariye, Ingila Sindaba … —the tiny girl, Maria … —Ingila Sindaba … our Maria … Ingila …

Ingila Sindaba. Immanuel was finished, shattered. He panted from the labour. Pulled up his mundu and got out. Mariakutty lay on the cold ground and chanted —Ingila Sindaba. She didn't know he had left. Her mind was at the hilltop. Life in hiding. Tears, like rain, a drop filled a pot. Little ones, four little ones. Scattered. Three were lost. Little Maria fell. Little Maria, who held out the light for Putuppally and Toppilaan. Little Maria, who had lisped and giggled, Ingila. Hungry, worn, crying, crying, crying, Mama, Mama, Mama, delirious little Maria. The police waited, she was the bait. At night Papa stole in. Swooped her up. Gave the slip to the police. A whole day and night inside the brushwood. He came, with dried blood stains all over. On Papa's shoulder lay Maria, like a wilted vine. Opened her eyes at Mama's touch. An upward glance, like the dying flame's leap. She was buried on the hilltop. The arrest came that night. The police growled all around the bottom of the hill—Mariakutty, don't give in. They'll catch me. Beat me up. Kick me. Even kill me, perhaps. But if I'm alive, I'll come back. You must hang on—I will, don't flinch. No, we'll all go. But the good time will come, it will.

Back at the village. Where it was home. No walls, door, just the foundation. The wife of Chorakkadan, murderer of six policemen. No warmth in anyone to offer a drink of water. No spunk to offer work. Only the police came. Six or seven, can't remember right. The blouse got torn off. The mundu flew off. The wailing baby flew, too. It broke its back on the hard ground outside. That infant never crawled on fours. Didn't sit. Walk. That's Lourdes. The kid who peed in laughter, in tears, in terror. Nothing to eat. To wear. Nothing to feed the half-paralysed baby sucking hard at shrunken breasts. The police came in turns. Handcuffed her, and then raped. She shut her eyes tight and prayed—Ingila Sindaba. They dipped the broken-down infant in water to produce different kinds

of screams. People gaped. Communist wench. Hardy
stuff. The ploughed-up soil sprouted. People laughed.
Did you hear? The wife of the jailed comrade is pregnant.
That's socialist pregnancy. Communist pregnancy. Just
wait, the kid's going be born with a hammer and a sickle.
She gave birth, all alone, inside a thatched parting. Cut
the umbilical cord by herself. A boy. The Virgin hath
given birth. He was named Immanuel.

No one would give her work. But visitors arrived
at night before the broken-down door of the house.
Chorakkadan's wife Mariakutty thus became socialist
Mariakutty. She wandered in search of her lost children.
Found them, in the end. Anna, at Alleppy. A servant in
a house. Mary, at Ambalappuzha. Begging. Anna came
running, shouting aloud, Mama, Mama … Mary stared
for a while. Then collapsed in a faint. Maggie wasn't
found. Lost, somewhere. Where? Taken by the beggars?
Thrust into some churchyard to beg, with legs broken,
eyes gouged? The womb burned. Nipples smouldered.
Maggie, Maria, babies borne in the womb all ten months.
Babies brought forth in pain. Babies fed at the breast to
the heart's content. Little fingers that caressed Mama's
face, and tiny mouths pressed around nipples. Tiny
mouths that pulled off the breast without warning and
shaped into roguish smiles. The marks of Papa's love.
The tokens of Mama's devotion. My Maggie, my Maria,

my Immanuel. Two years, thus. He came back. The man who went inside unbowed. He came out bowed, crooked. They looked at each other, intently, for a long time. His lips moved. She didn't hear. Maybe it was to call her, Mariye, my own. My Mariakutty, my jar of wine, my wine glass, maybe all this. Didn't hear. Mariakutty handed him the child. Chorakkodan took him. Pressed him to his chest. The husband broke down and wept. The wife murmured—Ingila Sindaba.

Immanuel walked to Moscow Junction, exhausted. The long grey hair swung, touching his shoulder. He scratched the bald patch, in between. Immanuel. He whispered. Bastard. The seed of six policemen. Six men. Immanuel spat out in hate. Revolution, his mother's cunt! Chorakkadan, son of a thief. Didn't let me call him Father. Called him Comrade, only that. Never called me son. Only Comrade. Grew up hearing a new story every birthday. People pointed out each of the six to him. Put bets on whose resemblance was clearest. As Immanuel grew, Chorakkadan waned. More of silence, less of talk. The night the Party split,* he got mightily drunk. Came home with a big bottle. Called to her one more time, Mariakutty, my own wine-jar. Cook me some tapioca. Told jokes from the lock-up. Described the different

---

* The Communist Party of India's split.

blows in jail. Relished Mariakutty's chilly-and-tapioca doused with oil. Got the kids together around him one last time. Caressed them all one last time. Kissed Mariakutty one last time. Lay dead the next day, blood seeping from the corner of his mouth.

Acchu's petty shop. Immanuel bought a bottle. The illicit stuff. Walked back, stuffing it in his mundu. His first drink was from what was left in the bottle Chorakkodan brought before his death. The first sip was sour. He felt, then, that it would be the last. Got a job in the factory. Fell in love with the girl who worked with him. Was shattered when she said, 'I don't want a bastard.' He went to a whore that night, in rage. When she shut the door and slipped off her clothes, he saw his mother. Six policemen. Mother, all alone. Mother, naked. Blood-soaked. The Ingila ... rang in his ears. He heard the infant's scream from the front yard. He ran out, frenzied. He tried again and again. Many experiments. Many whores. Women of many kinds. But when each woman shed her clothes, he collapsed. Was shattered in the dark, in the light, at night, in the day. Each time he went back to beat up Maria. Drank in the veranda till daybreak. Called Mama for company. Mariakutty came out, silent. In the white tin plate, there would be meat sometimes, sometimes fish. Or mangoes. Or just green chillies. Immanuel would stretch in the armchair. Sip his drink, slowly. Forget that he beat up his mother. Mother would forget the beating, too. Staring into the dark where the crickets raised slogans, Maria would wait. Then, gradually, he got off women. In between there was a strike in the factory. A lockout. He lost his job. Immanuel tried many things. Was never able to stick to anything. Never got a decent wage. Never managed a full stomach. Never calmed his mind. Wants lay stagnant. Whenever he saw a jatha, heard slogans or a speech, he went berserk. Maria would be pounded on those days.

The house was near. Immanuel flew into a rage, again. Thunder rang in his swollen feet, again. A storm gathered on his face. He jumped over the fence, into the veranda. Reached out for the Furedan, bought from Vijayan's manure shop. Shook half of it into the glass. Sat back in the armchair and called Mother. Maria, ten kilos heavy, eighty-nine years old, wobbled out. Pushed the last green chilly in the white tin plate to his feet. Immanuel took in his drink, drained out. Maria waited, silent. Everyone will forswear someone one day, before the cock crows. Everyone will crucify someone between two thieves, one day. Will make someone drink sour wine. Stab someone in the breast. Throw someone into a tomb carved in the boulders. At the door of the vault, some Maria alone will wait, weeping for the man she loved.

What the Souls Do at Midnight

Drives you crazy, this pest of a Soul!

Sarala Headmistress falls asleep—and hey, this Other-female, this sly Soul, wakes up.

Out of Mistress's ageing body—all of forty years—it emerges, stretching vigorously like a hunter waking in his riverside tent, throwing a contemptuous glance at the body, five feet long and some forty inches wide. The Body is but an Impermanent Garment. Nearly in tatters after much washing. Here it is—breasts flopping all over the chest, midriff loose and flabby, baggy cheeks on a sallow face. The hollow under the chin has collected quite a bit of fat. Below the eyes, dark patches have spread. Yessir, this thing is turning fusty. No point, really, in sending it to the laundry; better get a new one. As far as Soul is concerned, Mistress's body is like a nightgown. Good, no doubt, to put on. The more worn it is, the more comfortable. But worn, still. Can't wear it to go out—no sir, not at all.

So, as already stated: Other-female materializes. Its nightly jaunts are not new. Early on, they used to be around the house. The rice batter in the kitchen—hope the cockroaches weren't falling into it? Were the rats getting at the potatoes in the plastic basket? Has someone left the bathroom tap open? Those were the kinds of things Soul fretted about. But one night Mistress's Soul bumped right into her husband's Soul. That meeting was a bit of trouble; the latter was in a sort of tricky situation with the Soul of the woman next door. Mistress's Soul was really very hurt. The domestic outings ended then. Once night fell, once Mistress fell asleep, Soul would slink out like a cat. Through the bedroom door, footfalls muted, it would enter the passage. The eldest son's room is just opposite. This gentleman is a third-year graduate student of science. He has been provided with a computer, bought on a bank loan. The fellow's forever buried in his browsing. No worries on whether Mother has a soul, and if she has one, what it is up to. Even if he did, what did Soul care? Let him go and check in the bedroom. Mistress's body's lies there still, clad in a brown-coloured nightgown with big yellow-sunflower print, face resting on the left arm, mouth somewhat open, fast asleep.

The room next to it belongs to Mistress's second boy. This gentleman is in school—higher secondary. His breath stinks of tobacco. That's from smoking a leftover cigarette butt discarded by his father. Perfectly set under his pillow is an open page from a magazine carrying a brassiere advertisement. Studying remains the least of his interests. If it were somewhat otherwise, he would have surely managed a decent pass at least in one or two papers in the Onam exam.

Let that be. Now, as far as Soul is concerned, the tough part is getting past the boys' rooms. Once that is achieved, then it is downstairs, straightaway. There are three rooms downstairs: the sitting room, the dining room and the kitchen. The body of the husband, the once-head-constable-now-beefed-up-to-Circle Inspector, would be at rest in the sitting room, legs stretched on the divan, slurping up Fashion TV. The door is discreetly shut. Can't let the boys' studies suffer. Husband is an officer who sleeps little. His eyes are ever wide open. An extremely busy Soul. Therefore he never notices Mistress's Soul step out, nor does he hear the soft tinkling of the wind chimes over the doorstep when Soul brushes past it on its way out. In order to sense that something, he would have to know a bit of feng shui. But well—policemen? And feng shui? Ooh!

That's Mistress's great advantage vis-à-vis the Circle [Inspector]. She even knows about feng shui! What's the connection, you may ask, between Headmistresses and feng shui. True, under ordinary circumstances, Headmistresses need know nothing of feng shui. But they can't escape that knowledge in this New Age. These days we are being attacked by knowledge pouring in from all over. As a result, Headmistress too arrived at feng shui, step by step. Thanks to the headmaster of the Boys' High School, Janardana Kurup. It is true that the girls' and boys' schools are housed in separate buildings. But they have a common canteen. At noon, the mistresses and masters of the two schools congregate in this thatched shed for lunch. They have a separate space to themselves, properly private.

Headmaster spoke of world affairs during lunch hour. That is how Mistress got to know of the Pournami Service Society. That led her to become a pious participant in the mass prayer at the goddess' temple nearby on each full moon day. There she would be regularly, dressed in the traditional off-white two-piece sari. Soon, Master mentioned the Baba's wonderful acts.

Naturally, Mistress began to lean in that direction. She put up a big image of the Baba at home and worshipped it. Many things—honey, sacred ashes, milk, ghee—flowed miraculously from the image. Relatives, friends, Master himself, flocked there to witness the miracle. Another time Master talked of the sacred miracles at Vallikkavu. From then on, Mistress attended the devout Unions—the satsangs—along with Master. But the Art of Living became popular around that time. Then, for some days, every evening after school, both of them attended the Art of Living course. They reached home at dusk, smiling at each other, soaked in sweat, after all the prancing and dancing. Sugar and BP levels fell rather quickly. A general sense of well-being shaped up. And before long Master turned eloquent about Chinese astrology, feng shui.

'It's quite accurate, you know. Can't help believing. So many people's experiences …' one afternoon Master swore to Mistress. That made Mistress very keen. Laying two mattresses upon the same cot leads to marital disharmony, Master remarked. The very same day, Mistress removed the family cot from the bedroom and replaced it with individual cots, with individual mattresses and individual bedcovers. She then pushed them close together and perched a little statue of kissing doves at the head of the cots. Whenever it fell noisily to the floor knocked down by Circle in one of his fits of anger, she would always carefully and nervously restore it to its correct position at the head of the cots.

'There should be no mirrors in the bedroom,' Master said one day. 'Not just the mirror but every other shining object in the bedroom should be hidden under cloth curtains. Only then will there be happiness … energy … in the body … at daybreak.'

'What's the connection between mirror and energy?' Mistress sounded anxious.

'You wouldn't know! All of us have Souls in our bodies. These things step out of our bodies and wander around at night. In truth the dreams we see at night are the doings of the Souls, at night …'

Something sharp, almost a streak of lightning, passed through Mistress's forty-year-old body. For some days, she argued with herself: yes, no. And then compromised: maybe true, who knows? It bothered Mistress no end, like a troublemaker of a student who could not be dispatched with a TC. But soon the helpless conclusion was: oh yes, true, but who is bothered? The moment she conceded 'true', she was lost. Soul proclaimed Freedom. Without a care, it began its nightly excursions.

I have already told you, at midnight Mistress's Soul would cross her sons' and husband's rooms, traverse the front yard, open the gate and get out into the road. There, in street-lamp-light, it would don a fluttery moth-body. Bleak dark nights can make anyone feel lonely. Soul fluttered its wings to shrug off the heaviness. Then, soon, its translucent wings would droop and fall off. A worm-body stinking of stale oil would wriggle its way back. At dawn, the street lights blinked dead. Burning bright, even then, would be the pangs of loneliness. When she woke up at the sound of the alarm at six sharp, when she made black coffee and poured it into the thermos, sometimes, Mistress would catch a whiff of the scent of stale oil in a glass tumbler. Not recognizing it to be her own scent from the past night, she would wash the tumblers with soap, again and again.

And so this went on and on. Once, when Mistress was fluttering about in her moth-guise, she saw another Soul under the street lamp, alone and sorrowful. Like a school kid parted from its companions, it sat, sad, chin resting upon its hand. Mistress's Soul was pretty sure that no one would recognize her—that made her a bit bold and naughty. The kid ran after the moth. The innocent game was fun, but time flew, and the Soul-moth's wings would soon fall. Anxious now, Mistress tried to escape, flying off as fast as she could. The kid tried to grab her but got just one of her wings. Like Cinderella who ran off without her slipper before the magic time elapsed at twelve, Mistress escaped, flying now, falling now, but reaching home on one wing.

That day, at school, during lunch hour, Master said, 'Yesterday I had a strange dream. That Mistress had turned into a moth ... I tried to grab you and a wing came loose. When I woke up in the morning, there was this wing ...'

Master opened his purse and placed before her a crystal wing. Some vague memory made Mistress feel nervous and shy. That night, Mistress's Soul tried hard to pull off the single wing, like Cinderella's single slipper. Soul didn't feel brave enough to venture out. The body tossed and turned.

Circle had gone to sleep, content after reiterating in police language his long-standing views on the infamy that characterized three generations of Mistress's lineage and the dowry arrears he was yet to receive. In any case the man has more than one Soul. Each had gone its own way. Mistress tried hard to sleep. Soul's desolate single wing yearned to fly. It stumbled on the memory of the lost wing. Then, hey presto, there wafted in Master's Soul, a breath of fresh air. Tenderly holding out to her the lost wing. And Mistress's Soul, it demurred no more.

That was the time of the return-monsoon. The mild wetness of rain lingered on. The clouds practised their Art of Living high above. There unfolded the devout Union of the stars. The pious full moon doggedly pursued piety on sacred sky-paths, rolling around some divine sanctum in intense *sayanapradakshinam*. Mistress's and Master's Souls rose to celestial heights. Now clad in star-bodies that shimmered in the heights. Now in bright comet-bodies that zoomed around sky slopes. Now melting into the sea as ribbons of moonlight. Now reborn as octopuses, swimming out into the open deep. Around them swam nine carp fish, bringers of good luck. The carp were blue. With orange gills. Pink eyes. Sixteen octopus-arms held each other between the swimming fish. Swinging to and fro upon wave-boughs.

It was getting light. The sky grew pale, washed clean and soaked blue by the return-monsoon. The two Souls were still in floating octopus-bodies; now they woke up. The seawater felt softly warm at dawn. Fishing boats with whirring motors whizzed past. The stink of diesel filled air and water. Mistress's Soul held Master's Soul firmly with all eight arms. He tried to shake her loose.

'Ambujam will be up soon ...' he murmured.

Mistress felt sad. They had missed flitting about as mating doves. Hadn't donned dragon-bodies that spit fire.

'Ambujam will be up soon ...' Master sounded alarmed.

Circle, too, would be up soon. So will be the boys. Mistress let go. Octopus-bodies tumbled back, dead. The Souls got up from the sea and went home.

According to feng shui, no mirrors are to be placed in bedrooms. But Mistress's bedroom was indeed defective. The mirror-door-ed cupboard was built-in—couldn't be removed or covered up. Soul was blinded by the light from the mirror as it entered the room. It squirmed at the thought of getting in. Mistress's ugly and unshapely body lay reflected in the mirror. Wing-less. Gill-less. Leaf-less. Flower-less. Vim-less and vigour-less. A clumsy sack of leather all stuffed with fat. Soul felt puke-y. The sky, the sea, the soil, and the deep called to it from memory. It wanted to flee.

And if so? Headmistress won't wake up in the morning. She won't make black coffee and store it in the thermos; she won't dry-fry flour to make puttu for breakfast. The boys won't wake up to the sound of the chutney being ground in the mixer. Circle and sons will discover Headmistress's body clad in the sunflower-print nightie with its mouth slightly ajar in the bedroom with the mirror-door-ed cupboard. They will weep aloud, recalling her to be good and kind. Safe in the ignorance of the wanton acts of her Soul at midnight, they will pray for her rest. And Master, what will he do? Will he go to the school as if he knew nothing? Will he lead the mourners' procession to her house, wreath in hand, wearing a black badge? Will he speak in the condolence meeting, voice breaking with emotion? Too many bothersome things.

Soul felt bleak. Outside, it became quite bright. Souls, of course, do not travel after daybreak. What else to do? Soul donned Mistress's body, once again. The body woke up with a kind of depression that it often experienced on certain mornings, directed itself to the kitchen, entered into black coffee-puttu flour-lunch packets-processing activities.

Circle, who had helped himself to the black coffee, rubbed his tummy and went off for a walk. He returned with a kilo of fish.

Mistress stared into the plastic bag. Inside her, something jerked.

Carp, light blue in colour, orange gills. Exactly nine.

'Oh … aren't these those fishes?' Fishes fated to swim in the frying pan tonight. Mistress looked at them, anxious.

'Which fishes?' Circle had no clue.

'In last night's dream,' she was about to say. She couldn't. Other-female wouldn't let her.

Well, it was OK to say. How many people know the truth about dreams?

41

The Scent of News

That was an infernal stink. Like the scent of rotten flesh. Anna Santhosh Paul's nose, of twenty-six years' service, first got a hint, and then sought it out. Who could it be?

She studied it. Very faint. So it can't be a found-dead-in-his-house. Could well be a grandma with a rotten bedsore. Or maybe—though this was less likely—the keeper of some cemetery.

As she sought out space for another item in the last-edition page, Anna became sure: this scent is of one of those three. Then she waited, impatient, for the person bringing the news, who would answer the security guard's questions, get an entry pass, walk up the stairs.

Anna decided that she should, as usual, not look up when he came in. She would simply point to the chair and ask him to be seated. If she threw a sly sidelong glance, she would see the surprise in his face. Surprise at how she knew that he was coming without looking up, without him clearing his throat. Anna never paid attention to that surprise. Because she had been so used to seeing it on Santhosh's face.

Those were the days. When Anna used to hurry and wind up the third edition before three o'clock. Santhosh used to come over from the far corner of the newsroom, relieved of his shift as night editor, rubbing his sleep-weary eyes, the mild scent of Park Avenue shaving lotion wafting ahead of him. 'There's coffee in the thermos,' Anna would say, neither looking up nor turning her head away from the computer screen.

In the early days of their marriage Santhosh was always surprised by this. How do you know that I am coming without turning your head, he would ask. Whenever that question popped up, Anna would turn love-filled eyes towards him and say, 'That's what's called a nose for news!'

Anna scratched her nose intuitively. The scent came back. She knew that the scent would now be near the entrance counter, and past the security guard's questions. Anna didn't raise her head or look. She had two reasons for not doing so. One, news that was fated to come would come, no matter what. She was past the age in which one thought otherwise. Her forty-eighth birthday was last month. And second, the deadline for the fourth change was drawing close. As far as an editor is concerned, messing around with deadlines isn't an option in life.

'Give me a deadline,' Santhosh would ask those days, even if the trip was to the market. 'How late can I be?'

How can any life, any action, be meaningful, without a deadline? After Sunny was born, whenever there was a fuss about baths or meals, he would ask, 'OK, what's my deadline?'

Anna felt a sudden urge to wind up work. The truth was that these days, for some obscure reason, her last edition was always late. Take today's fourth-change page. It has no major changes worth noting. The ones that happened were minor: the replacement of Irulaankunnel Suryakumar of Thodupuzha (22) of the first change by Turulayil Vettikkuzhiyil Satyavan of Kochi (88) and the shifting of the late news about the purana-writer Paravoor S. Sankaradas to include Irulomattam Devasya (74) with the headline 'The new episcopa's older brother' in bold. All these were done soon after the second-edition page was released. But just as she was mulling over the possibility of getting a laser printout of the page and making corrections, the 'Woman found dead' made trouble.

That item was just above 'Kanjiramattam Panchaarakunnel Paulo', which was fifth in the third column. 'Kanjiramattam Panchaarakunnil Paulo (98) passed away ... Funeral service at Puthen Church, Kanjiramattam. The late Uppukuzhiyil Thekkedathu Maria was the wife of the deceased. Sons and daughters: Mathew (late), Leelamma (late), Annamma (late); sons-in-law and daughter-in-law: Sosa (late) (former judge, district sessions court), Alexander (late) (retired chief engineer, PWD), Napoleon (former DCC general secretary).' Paulo had been nailed within a box two and a half centimetres broad and two and a half centimetres long. In the first and second editions he had obediently stayed in his place. (Paulo had suffered from chronic diabetes in his last years. His body had become so soft that it bruised easily, and every bruise turned into a festering wound. Years of suffering, in the care of foul-mouthed home nurses.) When Anna's attention flagged for a second, Paulo plucked off the nails and jumped out. And let himself into that space—the '... found dead' bit.

The deadline was close now. She knew it even without looking at her watch. After being in this job for seven or eight years, she had learned to work without a watch. The deadline is a habit. One would be almost in frenzy if the page wasn't ready by that time. As if one was dying without a sip of water anywhere in sight.

Anna wanted a sip right then. Those days, Santhosh used to pour her coffee—she remembered though she didn't want to remember. Santhosh would sit in one of the visitors' chairs and pour out the coffee. Anna would take it, one hand still on the keyboard. As they sipped the coffee slowly, between three o'clock (when the third edition had to be closed) and four (when the fourth edition was finalized), Anna and Santhosh would talk of everyday things—the home loan, Sunny's schooling, the housekeeping bills—things serious and not so serious. Anna would edit the fourth-change page in between their talk; Santhosh would run his eyes on the laser prints and suggest corrections.

'I forgot to soak the rice and lentils. Shall we have bread for breakfast?' she would ask, carefully placing the deceased Veeran Koya of V.M. Manzil at the top-right corner of the obit page. Running his eyes over 'The cremation and funeral rites of the late Eerezha Manidumkuzhiyil Lakshmikutty Amma (90) will be held today', Santhosh would tell her, 'Oh … I forgot … We are out of Ammachi's medicine oil. Remind me to get some tomorrow …'

As she titled the proofread obit page 'Health Standing Committee Chairman of the City Corporation passes away', Santhosh would share a joke from the main desk, and amid the bursts of laughter Anna's hand would slip off the keyboard and the brackets put around the names of the Chairman's offspring would slip off too.

By the time Anna had released the last edition and sent a message to the pre-press, Santhosh would have gone downstairs and started up their motorbike. It would be cold. They would speed home in the chilly wind, or if it was rainy, through the streaks of rain falling like whiplashes. They would arrive shivering and Santhosh would collapse into bed, planting a kiss on their sleeping son's forehead and sighing, 'Ah, what does this guy know of the housekeeping struggles of a journalist couple!' or something to that effect. If Sunny had to go to school, Anna would set the timepiece for six o'clock, snuggle up beside Santhosh at the edge of their cot and shut her eyes for an hour. Santhosh smelled of third-edition proof-copy. The scent of hot news.

Anna looked at the screen. 'Woman Found Dead' was still in the same space. Kanjiramattathu Panchaarakunnil Paulo had climbed on top of Ponkunnam Navjivan Andrew Luka's son Aby Luka (two and a half). Anna caught hold of Paulo's ear, a bit irritated, pulled him down, and restored little Aby fondly to his little space.

'Trying to fool me, eh?' she smiled tenderly at Paulo. Each day, so many grandfathers, so many younger brothers, so many little ones, each day ... All of a sudden Anna realized how much she had changed in these twenty-six years.

The letter that arrived the third day after she received her doctorate in journalism said: 'We expect great things from Anna ... Therefore we entrust her with the most important page of our newspaper. We hope that she will rise to meet our expectations completely ...' It had left her feeling hopelessly tired.

'I can't ...' she had raged and wept before Santhosh, then just a boyfriend. 'The page of the dead ... I'll be scared ... I'll end up with nightmares ...'

'Don't be so weak, Anna,' Santhosh had chided her. 'A talented journalist has much to do even in an obit page.'

Aravindakshan Nair Sir, who had been in charge of the obit page for decades, was retiring. 'This discomfort is no discomfort at all, my dear,' he had said, trying to console Anna, who was in tears. 'Haven't you read the Bible? He does not take his riches with him in death; nor does his greatness follow him.'

Her protests did not stop even after he left. But one day she picked up the copies on the desk. Her hand stumbled on a colour photograph, in army uniform, with army medals. The news item was on his letter pad: below 'Col. (Ret.) R.P.P. Nambiar' printed in grand gold lettering was scribbled 'Vijayapuram: Col. (Ret.) R.P.P. Nambiar (87) passed away. A decorated soldier, he was awarded the President's Vishisht Seva Medal. Funeral ...'

Anna shook inwardly. The revelation was so forceful, so vivid. Later, when the news of the waste-paper merchant's death arrived scrawled on a piece of waste-paper, when the news of the doctor's demise was brought by his last patient, she felt the same intense shiver. How many different kinds of passing away—she discovered, in disbelief—loved, unloved, hated, rejected. Some in guilt; some, detached. She felt embarrassed about her own pain. What more have the living to say, than the dead?

The usual three-o'-clock breeze came in through the window. Anna felt strangely sleepy. She looked around, pushing back some stray grey strands and giving her face a firm rub. The room was empty. The white-painted curved desks resembled tombs without crosses.

Earlier, she used to try and free herself as soon as possible after finalizing the third matter, and making corrections in the fourth, and finding space for a picture of two and a half centimetres and news of three and a half at the top edge of the page. That was a precaution. There could be a bit of news, anywhere, any time. There's no news more important in life than that of somebody's death.

'Built the tomb?' Santhosh would ask when she relaxed, leaving the space at the page's top-edge. 'Hope the guy who comes fits in there.'

'Who exists in this world that can't be fitted into a three and a half centimetre news item a two and a half centimetre stamp-size?' Anna would open her nose.

'There—I am catching an NRI-death-scent.'

Santhosh was astonished that day when, without much delay, a group came in with the news of the death of an aged mother, of several NRIs . 'But do tell me, how did you know?'

'That's nose for news!' Anna laughed.

'Oh, indeed ... nose for news ... of the obit-page editor!' he mocked.

Anna hasn't forgotten that day. That was the last day. Never again did she finish work on the third matter hurriedly; never could she sit back and chat with him. The next day, Santhosh was transferred to Delhi for small-talking too much with his wife after duty hours.

'What a life ...' Anna had sniffled, as Santhosh packed his suitcase. 'I've had enough.'

'How can you say that?' he tried to prevail upon her. 'We'll give a request when the general transfers are due. It's just a matter of finding a school for Sunny, isn't it?'

She wiped her eyes. In the days that followed, when Sunny cried for Appa, she would describe to him the school he would go to in Delhi. The flat they would live in ... all the wonderful things they would do.

Anna suddenly remembered the deadline. Why was the news taking so long, why had it not reached her? She felt rather overwhelmed. If there was no news, she could go home and press Sunny's clothes for college. But the scent of the news had indeed wafted upstairs ... she fretted.

Oh, what's the nose for news to an obit-page editor?

For a moment Anna thought she was hearing Santhosh's voice. Like a nail come loose on the lid of a coffin, it rattled in her mind.

That was when news arrived of Santhosh's moving to another newspaper after five years in Delhi. By that time letters, phone calls, visits, and gifts and messages for Sunny were few.

'Shall ... shall I come too?' Anna had asked, fumbling for words. 'How can I ... here?'

'Well ... what's to come of that?' She smelt the remoteness in his voice. 'Nobody can survive here on one person's salary.'

'Can't I find a job there?' she'd asked, despondent.

'Find a job, indeed! What's your experience? Eight or ten years on the obit page?' He laughed the murderer's cruel laugh.

The Scent of News

You handle the obit page, how can you be called a journalist? That was Santhosh's question. Am I not a journalist? Anna's self-respect was hurt. The only quality of a journalist is a nose for news, right, she asked herself fervently. It was with that doggedness that she specialized in the many scents of news.

On the day she picked up the write-up about Chettukuzhiyil Raghavan's death, she crinkled her nose and exclaimed about 'the smell of spirits'.

'Well, that ...' the agent smiled, searching for the photograph of the deceased in his bundle of news items. 'Wasn't Raghavan chetan the best-known hooch-maker in that area?'

That was the start. Later, Anna got the scent of sweet-cigars as she read of the demise of Elakkattil Elyamma (78). The agent confirmed that she used to be a cigar-seller. The passing of Ravuther of Ramapuram smelt like raw iron. It was mentioned later that he was an iron merchant in town. It didn't stop there. When the news write-up about Kalthottil Cheriyan K. Cheriyan's departure was opened, there rose up the myriad scents of all the liquors he had drunk, all the food he had feasted on, and the women he had slept with. From Panaikkaamala Saradaamma's death-news wafted the scent of all the country hooch and mango pickle eaten by her husband that spread in the air as he pummelled her on

55

the backside. And from Thelakkaattil Kunhonacchan's, the scent of a pillow gone musty with all the tears shed over a wife who had eloped.

Helpless, she came to terms with some stark truths. One, just because it looked unbelievable, news didn't become non-news. Two, all news is written in advance. The competent journalist got to it sooner.

Anna felt that someone was coming up the stairs. She abruptly retuned to reality. That news, it is coming. She put on the serious expression becoming of a journalist, turned her face towards the computer screen and privately followed the scent. A faint smell of rot. She thought hard: Who could that be?

It was the scent of Park Avenue lotion that entered her nostrils. She trembled. Her nostrils opened wider. Did she catch a whiff of Poison by its side? No. She will never be bold enough to appear before me, Anna gritted her teeth. She remembered the line from the Bible, he who abandons his wife for another woman commits adultery against her. As she remembered the line, as always, her hands sought out the Bible. Unable to find it, she muttered her usual sentences. Mark 9:43: 'And if thy hand offend thee, cut it off: it is better for thee to enter into life maimed, than having two hands to go into hell, into the fire that never shall be quenched.'

Anna shivered mildly as she felt a hand on her shoulder. She turned around.

'Ammachi,' Sunny suppressed a yawn and tried to smile. 'Don't want to sleep?'

'Without sending off the page?' Anna laughed as if he had cracked a joke. 'There's a final change to the last edition. How can Ammachi come without making that?'

'There's no change to the last edition, Ammachi,' Sunny suppressed another yawn. 'There's no more news to come.'

Sunny caught hold of her hands and raised her to her feet. Then he gently steered her forward, away from the obituary notices.

'But ... Son ...' Anna's nostrils were busy as she collapsed, drained out, into bed. 'Hey, here again ... that faint rotting stink ...'

Sunny didn't speak. He bent down, examining Ammachi's left calf. And then his nose for news chimed:

'Journalist Anna Santhosh Paul found fettered, rotting ...'

A Cat, Utterly Personal

His heart trembled as he watched her open the glass door of the cabin. She hesitated for a moment at the opened door. Blinking kitten-eyes surveyed him. The cat stepped out of her on four soft feet. It walked towards him, silently screaming love-me-please, tail aloft, eyelids quivering as if in a stupor. Throwing a silent challenge, it pressed against his calves: even if you don't love me, I will love you. It then settled on his feet submissively. He wanted to beg, please call it back before the all-seeing eyes of office superiors reach here. He couldn't even raise his head, though. And so he searched hurriedly for a piece of paper that wasn't in the file.

The papers were either in the Managing Director's file or in the General Manager's. The MD was seated to his right and the GM to his left. He had read them many times. They spoke of two kinds of bad conduct: one, guilty of negligence at work. Was supposed to go to Thiruvananthapuram for fieldwork but was found in Kozhikode. Second, moral negligence. Her arrest in a police raid has tarnished the institution's good name.

'Excuse me …' He caught the affectionate tone in her voice. 'May I come in, Sir?'

'You may …' It was the Managing Director who replied.

She shut the glass door gently and walked in. Through a corner of his eye he saw—she was wearing a sari with black-and-white checks and a white blouse. His heart pounded.

Though he wasn't looking up, he could sense the rhythm of her cat-like walk. He was scared. Will the white-furred cat spring up from inside her if he raised his eyes? These days, he was afraid of that cat. It sprang up at the merest sound of his voice. If he went closer, it would stretch, emit a mild purr and get to its feet. While she wore a sari, put up her hair, donned a middle-aged woman's serious demeanour, calculated turnovers and net profit, the cat would begin its own play, as if none of this mattered to it. A low miao. The ever-so-slight arching of the back, the swish of the tail and—the mildly adoring glance. Out, then, of her in a quick bound and, free-flowing, into him. He would be ordered: fondle me now. The truth is that in the early days he used to submit to this with an ardour quite unbecoming of a Deputy General Manager. Cats are irksome, especially in one particular way. If you start fondling them, you will have to do it forever. If not, they'll wander—without even the thought that this is a multinational company—around the office room and premises. Will go shamelessly on strike for a caress or cuddle. Even enter your bedroom. Push your wife to one side for space. Assert ownership by cuddling up against your chest. Once that stage arrives, there are just two things you can do—either kick it out heartlessly, or pick it up, hold it close to your chest, and walk out yourself.

His glance strayed for a moment towards her—she was sitting in a lone chair a little away from the glass-topped table. He withdrew at once and turned it on the GM. His face was full of sorrow. That didn't surprise him. That's how the GM always looked, on occasions like these.

'Suchitra, how is your father?' GM asked.

'Acchan's still the same, Sir,' he heard her reply politely. By 'Acchan' she meant a wizened, blackened skeleton. He had seen that man once. On the way back from a colleague's funeral together, he had visited her house. A house set with wooden window-bars shaped like stretched-out triangles. The skeleton was in a stuffy inner room filled with the scent of rot. The face had two naked white circles; the eyeballs had long retired beneath the eyelids, tired of sight. Acchan has been paralysed for years, she said, because of high blood pressure.

'Amma' was another, slightly less-decayed skeleton. She looked as if she had never smiled even once in her whole life. She slid in noiselessly with a cup of tea. When it was time to leave she called her daughter aside and spoke in a low rasping voice. Her face or voice betrayed no signs of love or tenderness towards her daughter. He saw her open her bag, fish out money and then rummage through all its pockets until some sum got put together.

As they were returning, she asked him to stop by the small junction. She got out, crossed the road and entered a phone booth. Two minutes later, she came out accompanied by a bloated-looking woman. As she took leave, she uttered some words, wiped her eyes. That's my sister, she said, as she got into the car. He saw her up close as they reversed. Her face was swollen, ill. That's because she has missed dialysis, she revealed casually, later. He could never understand how she managed to go to college and complete studies from this wretched home. He asked once, but she looked ready to burst into tears.

'Suchitra, we wanted to see you ...' he heard the Managing Director's voice again. 'Do you know what our greatest asset is?'

Off his guard for a moment, he looked at her face. That exact moment, she looked into his eyes. His body felt weak. His throat dried up.

It all began the night he was returning after arranging for his daughter's admission. She was also travelling in the Second Class AC compartment. She had been on fieldwork in the same city. It was she who asked the TTE for two adjacent berths. She talked for a long time into the night. Talking about life, she wept. Weeping women always made him feel sorry. All that he remembered was that he had tried to console her. The cat bounded towards him soundlessly without any warning. Weightless, like a bundle of peacock feathers. It rubbed against his feet, begging for love. He held it close to his chest.

'The dignity of this institution is very important to us, Suchitra. Therefore we are forced to take some truly unpleasant decisions.' The GM was speaking now.

The MD had spoken the same sentences to him earlier.

'What do you mean, Das? What about your family, your reputation, your social standing ... and above all, your wife's family ... their prestige?'

GM contributed the rest. Don't be a fool, Das. She's trapping you. She's the penniless sort ... the kind who seduces senior officers and ... —he offered instructions, what all had to be done. He took down the exact wording.

At night, he felt drained out. His wife's and children's faces glimmered in his memory. And then, the face of the skeleton in that house of wooden bars, with empty, ball-less eyes. She came in when he was waiting, lost in his thoughts, in the bedroom of the empty house, pen and paper ready on the bedside table.

'A letter ... just a formality ...' he remembered how he had tried to persuade her gently.

'I'm not writing. I need this job ...,' she had been stubborn. 'If we have an affair, that's our personal thing. Who has the power to interfere in that?'

He couldn't argue with her. Cuddling—that's the way to mollify any cat. 'As you say, Sir ...' she yielded. 'What should I write?'

There was just once sentence: 'Due to reasons that are utterly personal ...'

And did she write? 'Sir, for reasons that are utterly personal, I adore your eyes. They are like two glossy-plumed peacocks. Can't help this ... when they glance at me they open wide and graceful, like peacock plumes before rain clouds ...' Even otherwise, she is the brash sort. Doesn't obey easily. Keeps testing. The love, the forbearance, patience, of others ...

'This is the trouble with women,' he spit out, angrily throwing the crumpled piece of her writing into the dustbin. 'They have no prudence. Especially in relationships ...'

'This is the trouble with men.' She laughed. 'They are always senior officers—everywhere.'

For some time she lay prostrate on the bed, thinking. Then, got up and wrote another letter and signed it. Slipped it into an envelope and scribbled the address on it.

'We are not asking who you were with. Whoever that was, he can't be blamed. You should have been careful, Suchitra. After all, being a woman ...' bristling with indignation, GM abruptly turned to him.

'Why ... doesn't Ramadas have anything to say?'

He took off his glasses and looked up. Her kitten-eyes gleamed for him. The cat came out of her eyes—an ashen, icy, bloodless cat, cornered by hunting dogs. The oily black nose-tip glinted moist. The whiskers quivered sweet and vulnerable.

'If I lose my job ...' He remembered how her voice had broken when she had handed him the sealed letter.

A mass suicide. She probably wanted to say something like that.

'Ah ... don't worry ... I'm around, am I not?' He had caressed her head. Kissed her gently on the forehead. She reclined on his shoulder with a purr. She was his direct subordinate in the office. The final decision would be the DGM's. She joked weakly about the co-defendant proclaiming judgment. Took relief in the fact that his name had been omitted in the news report on the raid.

'Ramadas ...' GM was calling him now. He suddenly remembered that the GM was awaiting a response to his question.

'Our dignity, prestige, integrity ...' He hardened his voice. 'Anything else could have been forgiven ...'

Green eyes looked startled. He could see it rise to its feet, claws bare, back arched stiff, fur bristling.

'Let us accept the resignation.' Anxious to escape, he pronounced judgment.

'We have no choice.'

He felt that the cat was steaming as if it had fallen into hot water. Its fur was losing sheen, turning yellow. The moist black under the nose was dissolving to show the tiny bone below. The bright balls had dissolved into the eyes, leaving two grey holes. But even then, he asked himself, vexed, hell, why was this thing still crawling towards my feet?

She stood up. Kitten-eyes purred shut. She bade no farewell. Looked at no one.

When the glass door shut gently behind her, GM broke into a smile of relief.

'There—it went off smooth ... Now you can safely send for your wife ...'

He felt a wet cotton bundle lying at his feet. Don't cats die? He doubted. Even if they do, don't all cats have six or seven lives?

'I can't stand light-eyed women.' MD was saying. 'Haven't you heard? Light-eyed ones have more brains.'

'Not just brains, Sir,' he laughed and winked.

MD caught the allusion and guffawed. A moment later, GM, too.

As they roared with laughter together, the superiors may have noticed him press down his shoe, as if to crush something underfoot, on nothing. But they didn't ask.

Who doesn't have, in many things, some personal reasons?

Same-Sex Sorrows

The Phallus constitutes the Central Shaft, the very Axis of contemporary systems of power; it must be debilitated, demolished, destroyed without delay! Until he heard some women (whose bodies resembled dried-up twigs) hold forth like this at the women's seminar, microphone operator Gopalakrishna Pillai was an utterly banal Gopalakrishna Pillai.

He woke up in the morning. Drank black coffee. Damn, it wasn't sweet enough—flung a daughter-of-a-swine at Saraswati. Drew up water from the well, bathed. Broke the chilly into leftover rice gruel and swallowed it. Slipped into the three-days'-dirt-and-sweat-smeared brown-striped shirt. Draped the four-days'-muck-streaked saffron mundu. Put on the yellow plastic slippers frayed on many sides. Stepped out. Then Older Daughter asked for money for annual exam fees. Called her choicest names. Younger Son complained about not having a pencil. Raised a hand to slap him. Spit hard on the ground. In the kitchen, Saraswati threw a fit. In the middle of it, parted the fence and stepped into the road. Jumped on the first Ordinary bus to Thirvanthoram town. Climbed up the wooden staircase to the little room with the signboard 'Microphone for rent' above Guruvaayoorappan Hotel at Gandhari Amman Junction. Collected the microphone set. Flagged down an autorickshaw and climbed in. Reached the seminar hall at the Government Guest House. Connected microphones and speakers. Checked the wire connection. Shouted allo, allo, mic-T-Testing and was satisfied. Inserted a cassette into the player and curled on the chair in the microphone-corner. *Pineapple-girl-hey-choc-late-piece-hey* … blared. Lakshmikutty wafted into the mind along with Pineapple. Oh, forgot the fifty-rupee-balance there—felt flustered. Brightened up in the hope of borrowing the same from Pathrose the microphone owner. Dimmed in the fear that he would say no. Went out to the workers' toilet, smoked a Dinesh beedi, returned to the mic-corner. Waited impatiently for the function to begin. Then *Don't-like-you-fellow-I-don't-like-you-fellow* began. Naturally, Saraswati wobbled in. The delicious bait of dowry that her old man had once dangled popped up. Rage boiled with cuss words in the mouth. The body quivered in wrath. Got up, scratched the scalp, re-draped the mundu, and sat down hard on the chair again. Yes, a very ordinary Gopalakrishna Pillai. Or, the usual Gopalakrishna Pillai.

At that point, the meeting began. There was no prayer-song. The females stood up for a minute. Many kinds of females. Of many ages. Some in saris, some in pyjama-pants, some in skirts. Speeches marched on in a straight path. Women's speeches. Bother! Gopalakrishna Pillai yawned big as he adjusted the volume. In between two tall ones came up. Raised up the mic a bit for them. All thin as reeds. Not one to hold a candle to Lakshmikutty. Saraswati was so much better than these. Gopalakrishna Pillai was drowsy. And then she got up. A small little thing. Full-skirt of silk, eardrops, gold locket. Sort of reminded you of Older Daughter. Older Daughter had started her monthlies last year. A bit bigger than this one if she put on a skirt. Two or three years. Then she'll have to be married off. How? Something flared inside. In the middle, the skirted girl came up. Gopalakrishna Pillai got up to lower the mic. She ignored him and started

75

speaking. Didn't bother to listen to the beginning. But then 'Phallus' sounded in the ear. Gopalakrishna Pillai started: Good God, really, 'Phallus', the dick? Couldn't believe his ears and so hung on now. Yes, right, that was 'Phallus', the dick! Oof! He shrivelled.

The girl fumed ahead full speed. Squeaky-chick-like voice, but what a scowl, as fierce as a lion! It is the Phallus-dick that rules the land. Men are overpowering women and establishing sexual domination. The Phallus is a symbol. The cornerstone of today's rotten system of power and authority. The Central Shaft. Men are asserting sexual domination over women's identity. Every man, essentially, is a rapist! His natural tendency is to assault and conquer. No woman desires men. She is forced to submit. Women's sexuality is his concession, his favour. Is there any woman in this state who isn't sick and tired of suffering men's bad breath and sweat-stink?

Gopalakrishna Pillai's eyes popped. Good Lord! He jumped up almost unknowingly. Retied his mundu tighter. The leftover rice gruel boiled in his belly. He went out and paced up and down, rather uneasy. Words heaved up and down his gullet. Some fifty women were in the hall—the single male was he. The mentioned object would be found solely on his person! What an insult at this age of forty-five! What trouble! Gopalakrishna Pillai glanced at the women in the hall. Arseholes, shitbags!

Didn't they have men at home? Don't those fellows have arms and legs that work? He remembered his daughter again. Felt that she was up there. That she was making the speech. Ooh, how the blood frothed! His hands itched to lift up that skirt and cane her solid on the buttocks. This is a different bug! Steam escaped from the body boiling in rage. Walk, sit, kick—he wanted to do all this at once. He looked at the girl with gritted teeth. Her skirt! Dangling earrings! Break the Shaft, indeed! Tall stuff! Just you try, you little runt! The girl was still holding forth about Shaft-breaking. She is going to break the mic in her fit, Gopalakrishna Pillai feared. He said to her from inside, Ah, you break it, and that's going to be your very last.

The speech was over. The women took their TA and left. Gopalakrishna Pillai sat still, worn out. How sad. How disheartening. Numb at heart, he pulled out the mic connection. He remembered the Shaft when he saw the mic. He was washed out by the time he reached Swamy's Café via Thampanoor. He didn't ask Pathrose for money. But Pathrose sensed it. This isn't the usual Gopalakrishna Pillai. Not the normal one. Aren't you feeling well, Pillaicchaa, he asked. He handed some money for medicine, a fifty. Gopalakrishna Pillai took it reluctantly. He looked at Pathrose with sympathy. Another Shaft, he sighed at heart.

77

Sitting in the bus, he pondered. Really, was it all true? Will these wretches really break it? And will men hang around simply watching? Gopalakrishna Pillai spit hard. Don't let them study. The problem is too much study. These swine should be chained in the house. Don't let them loose. This is what letting them out leads to. Got off at Kesaasapuram. Walked towards the seedy area where his house stood. Bought a packet of arrack from Vattappaara's shop. Saraswati wasn't home from work. Fished out the key from above the door and entered the house. The place reeked of poverty. Lacks and wants hung grey. He poured himself a glass of arrack. He felt hungry. The kitchen was bare. He remembered that Saraswati had told him that they had no rice. Damn. Her stinking mother's rice. Let her get it if she wants. First get the dowry. Ha, you want to break it too? Try, you runt. He lay on the cheap coir cot for some more time. The seminar hall came back to his mind. All those women. The bangles, the chains, silk, flowers, perfume. Curs. Ought to be properly thrashed on the back and the middle. Ought to break their legs and drag them into a corner. Break the Shaft, indeed! God, what times, these! Would women behave like this in the past? Would they openly say Phallus-dick? Would they pour such scorn on men? Whatever wrong did men ever do to these females?

Saraswati came in then. The nasty boor's home early, she murmured. In time for lunch? She poked him. Gopalakrishna Pillai raised his head but was silent. Hey, this isn't my usual husband, a streak of lightning lit up Saraswati's brains. Her heart melted somewhat. 'Why, you sick?' She asked in slightly prolonged tones. He was hesitant but told her the whole story. Told her all about the speech. Some words, she couldn't make out. Those he explained as well as he could. Too bad if it is broke, she spewed, fellow can't even feed the kids he made, why he lug this around? Go ask your bitch, she poked him harder. Gopalakrishna Pillai blew up. His hopes about Saraswati had ended. The seminar came into his mind again. He remembered each female face there. Meditating on each of those, he worshipped Saraswati. Blows landed on her back and stomach. Ooh, ayyoo! The fucking monster's killing me, Saraswati screamed. Breaking the damn thing not enough, you wretch, she cursed; smash, grind, pound it deep inside the ground. That made Gopalakrishna Pillai go weak again. He aimed another kick at Saraswati wailing in the kitchen, and got out. Retied the mundu and walked on briskly.

Lakshmikutty. A little yard bordered by screw pine. A little hut. A yellow plastic line was strung in front of the house. Upon it lay a freshly washed red lungi and blue blouse. The thatched door was open. That's a sign—Lakshmikutty was there, and by herself. He went in, shutting the door behind. She came from within the thatched hut. His old flame. Lost her in the middle. Saraswati intruded in between. The bother had been loaded on his back. Lakshmikutty came to him cooing, Ooh, it is you, Anna! Had lunch, Anna? she asked caressingly. Gopalakrishna Pillai turned soft, weak. Lakshmikutty tucked the lower edge of the blue lungi below her ample waist, took off the towel from her breasts, threw it on the clothesline, and laid out the mat. In between she hinted at the fifty-rupee arrear from the last two times. He paid thirty for this time. She locked it in the cupboard. Came close smiling her deadly smile. Why you looking so strange, she asked. Gopalakrishna Pillai felt feeble. Darling, come here, he called, let me ask, you tell, what you feel about me? You love or hate? Ah, why this in your mind, Anna? Gopalakrishna Pillai told her the whole story. Now tell me, you been angry at me like that ever? Lakshmikutty let off peals of laughter. Oh no, did those dames tell this all, Anna? I tell you one thing. Listen, most men very bad. All men not good as you. Some men's—aw, really feel like breaking their things! So you never got any good feeling from all these men, Lakshmikutty? Aw, what feeling, Anna, the feeling is in the money. Lie down this side. I have to go to market today evening.

Gopalakrishna Pillai, poor soul. The Shaft of hope snapped. God, what a world. What a waste, these forty-five years. Nobody's happy. These females aren't what they look like. This is what is in their minds. Venomous creatures. Laughter and play, all put-on acts! He got up. Anna, Anna, Lakshmikutty's voice trailed behind. He didn't stop. Crossing the screw pine border, a thorn scratched his leg. The arrack burned in his stomach. Gopalakrishna Pillai walked on, hapless.

His legs carried him to Kesavadasapuram and stopped there. The speech still rang inside him. Older Daughter Sreelakshmi appeared before him in a silk full-skirt. She stood before the mic, complete with eardrops and locket. Break the Phallus, she squeaked like a chicken. Gopalakrishna Pillai muttered cuss words which slurred all over. So many men on the road. Men going home from office. Men getting back after hospital visits. Proudly parading their wives around. Pressing close to girlfriends. Gopalakrishna Pillai opened his blind-drunk eyes and looked around. The Shafts of Power. He empathized and sympathized. Poor things. How they live on, totally innocent. Smiling. Dashing about for their families. Walking on, dreaming. Dreaming of who? Chatting in sheer delight over the mobile phone? To who? Troubling themselves for somebody? For who? Gopalakrishna Pillai wanted to give them all a good beating. He stood there for some more time, calling women bad names. Declaring the fathers and husbands of all the women in the seminar hall impotent beggars. When it all thinned into a mumble, sat down in the veranda of a closed shop opposite Arya's Restaurant.

It got darker and darker. A young fellow in an orange T-shirt and single mundu sat down next to him and dropped a shy smile. Gopalakrishna Pillai didn't get the hint for a minute. His mind was full of women. Saraswati and Lakshmikutty. He remembered all the women he had slept with in and around town, and all the women who spoke at the seminar. Bloody corpses, he mumbled at heart. Why, Anna, you look sad? the young fellow asked. Gopalakrishna Pillai noticed him then. Twenty-five or twenty-six he would be. The lights began to go off in the shops. The young chap moved closer. Bit his nails, cast loving glances. Gopalakrishna Pillai burst into tears. The young chap started. Anna, oh, why you crying, he asked. Gopalakrishna Pillai sobbed and sobbed. In between told him the whole story. The story of the Shaft. Of the skirted-girl's speech. Tell me, fellow, wasn't that the cheek? The young fellow thought about it. Pulling up his bracelet the way girls pull back their bangles, he said, Anna, it isn't as you say. All I want is to be a girl. Have to make money like this somehow, have operation to become girl. Then, Anna, will you marry me, please?

Finally, *Sasandeham*

Something happened at Fantasy Park. Who knows what. Four or five days later, Sreekumari Amma became pregnant. What sort of pregnancy? Well, sincere, serious, not wilful but totally mature pregnancy. Her body bulged like a soaked green-gram seed. Her lower belly protruded, as if ready to sprout. As she got up from bed, her head spinned. Nausea welled up in her throat. Bile spouted into her mouth. Her legs wobbled. The body felt sapped.

She first thought it was gas. Sat on the bed, tried to burp once or twice. Indeed. When did the Belly ever recede with burping? Sreekumari Amma got up. Walked to the bathroom. As she washed her face after brushing, the first kick was delivered on the left side of her belly. Terrified, she pressed her stomach hard. But oh, in her palm she felt the heartbeat of the fellow inside. She was startled. To make sure it was true, she undid her mundu, pushed aside the neryatu, and checked. The belly was well advanced. Thunder boomed inside Sreekumari Amma, MA Malayalam, Mother-of-Three's head. Lightning flashed too. Is this not the same as that? The experience of being in the adventure ride Crazy Love in the Malampuzha Fantasy Park engulfed her once again that moment. There she was, flying high, turning head over heels in the air. The whole world spun around in the furious wind. Her ears were blocked. Darkness filled her eyes.

She hadn't wanted to go. It was her grandchildren. Her children had made plans to worship at Guruvayoor and then go to Malampuzha. They didn't want Amma to be left all alone. Sreekumari Amma was also keen on sightseeing. That is how she went to Fantasy Park. There was a lot of walking around. Her legs ached; she sat down on a cement bench when she saw one. Sons, daughter, son-in-law, daughters-in-law and the kids broke up into smaller groups or wandered off by themselves. Sreekumari Amma was sitting right in front of a ride called Crazy Love. Double chairs fixed on big cranes. When the ride began the chairs would rise up high in the air and rock like cradles. Then they would spin. The spinning would get faster a little later. And then they would swing up, down, left, right, and then turn over, upside down. The smiles on the faces of the riders would slowly fade, and alarm and anxiety would take their place. At the height of the turning-upside-down, loud ayyooo-s and please-let-me-down-s would rent the air. The way the pairs of riders get out when the ride ends is a sight to see. Undone hairdos, reddened faces, panting breath, shouts and screams, heaves of relief … onlookers would die laughing. This won't happen when we ride, they boast. But the same thing will happen to us. Sreekumari Amma too was in splits. She was sitting there rocking with laughter, shedding tears of mirth, when He came. They saw each other. Memories, delusion, all evoked by the resemblance. She suddenly remembered the MA Malayalam lecture class: Figures of Speech. *Smrithimaan*: Resemblance of one to another evokes memory. *Bhraanthimaan*: Resemblance of one to another evokes delusion. And finally, *Sasandeham*: Resemblance evokes *sandeham*—ambiguity, ambivalent feelings … They brushed away aches and age, and found each other. He held her right hand like in the MA days, with an even greater tremble of tenderness laced with hesitation. Sreekumari Amma blushed deeper than then; became sad, shed tears.

Right then, the volunteer getting people to take a ride on Crazy Love came up to them. He insisted. 'Oh, I don't want to,' she was reluctant. But He insisted, too. Don't you want to know what it is like sometime in this life? He gently teased. In the end she gave in. She put on the seatbelt of the iron chair, held tight to the iron bar in front. The chair rose up. God Guruvayoorappa, will the kids see me, she was anxious. Oh, what now if they do, he laughed. It was then he reminded her of Kannan. That was the pet name they wanted to give their child, the child of their dreams of those days. Oh, of those days. Her eyes brimmed with tears and sadness. He then took her wrinkled hand in his wide palm and held it firmly. Two hands, like crumpled cardboard pieces. Kannan's form flashed in Sreekumary Amma's mind. Only if it were this man, alive and well, and not the other, dead and gone; only if little Kannan was born—the thought shimmered in her mind for a moment. That was it. That was all.

The Crazy Love ride began in earnest. The chairs zoomed up together. They felt as if they were raised right up to the high heavens. He too rolled in the chair. 'Oooh—Stop! Let us out!' They heard many people scream. He was holding fast to Sreekumari Amma's hand.

At first her head went round and round. Then her breath was short. Finally, they came down, quavering. The chairs turned in circles. Head over heels. MA Malayalam lecture class: Poetic Metres—slow, fast-playful, faster-playful, wildly playful. *Keka, Kaakali, Drutakaakali, Mathebhavikriditham*. When they got off, their eyes were wet. Suddenly, Sreekumari Amma threw up. He got her a bottle of water and rubbed her spine gently as she puked in the washroom of the restaurant. She spun around, amazed. In his tired eyes she spied the tender glance of the old classmate from MA. Sreekumari Amma's body burst into a thrill even at her age.

Precisely then the children returned and were bewildered by Mother's sudden nausea. Sumitha was the doctor, she took over. Checked Mother's pulse quickly. Nothing's wrong, she said. Sreekumari Amma washed her face and looked around: He was nowhere to be seen. She looked inside, outside, in front of, behind the restaurant. He wasn't anywhere. How did He disappear so fast, she was stunned, just like in those days. Did you see the person who was standing here, she asked her children. None of them had seen anyone. They hadn't noticed. She sought Him everywhere right till they were finished and ready to return. She couldn't find Him anywhere. Sreekumati Amma can't make anything out of it. Did he come there? Or was it a dream?

So, is this belly a dream too? Doubt struck her. Sreekumari Amma pinched her body, nipped and tweaked harder. But—she felt a kick inside the second time. She swayed; it was a strong kick. No, this wasn't a dream. It wasn't? Wasn't it? How could a belly non-existent till yesterday pop up today? She poured some water on her face. No, this was no dream: Absurd Hyperbole. She came out of the bathroom slowly. Somehow crept up to the dining hall. By then her bones had begun to tinge and ache. A sea roared inside her middle. Waves of pain. Her spine began to tingle. She couldn't stand or walk. Sit or lie down. Sreekumari Amma panicked. Struggling to establish that all this was simply not true, she managed to feebly call Malini. It was really feeble, strangled. But good luck, Malini heard her call. She ran in seeing her mother-in-law hold on to her tummy and looking strange.

At first glance, she thought it was an attack, a heart attack.

'Ayyo ... chetta ... quick ... Amma's sick ... !' she yelled. 'What happened to Amma?' Satish jumped up, worried. 'Ammoomaa!' Achu and Kichu squealed. 'Go get some water ... Amma's soaked in sweat ...' Satish went wild. Sreekumari Amma was panting hard. Inside her chest, Baby Kannan was turning at wild speed, like on the Crazy Love machine. Son and daughter-in-law sprinkled water on her face again and again. As the cold water hit her face, Sreekumari Amma opened her eyes, which were shutting in sheer agony, with difficulty. The light was blinding. Satish's face was visible but blurred. Not the Satish with his late dad's six feet height and thick moustache but a newborn babe. Born just a few minutes ago. Its eyes weren't open. It hadn't yet learned how to make a sound. It was opening the mouth weakly as if to cry. Something heaved in Sreekumari Amma's chest. She felt her fallen breasts rise and firm up. To use a simile, like the way empty balloons fill up. The flesh thickened. Milk oozed. Not a dream. The truth. And besides, this was indeed that.

'Mother, shall we go to the doctor?' she heard Satish's anxious voice; but words stuck in her throat when she looked at his face. She ached, unable to utter a word, feeling like an offender. What was she to say, anyway? She had grown old. Her husband had died in her best years. His death was dying-in-harness and so she got a job. But raising three kids was tough on her. At last the kids were grown up. The boys became engineers, the girl, a doctor. After retiring as a high-school teacher, Sreekumari Amma ought to have spent the rest of her days in a life befitting her age and health, offering whatever help she could, avoiding as much bother as she could, praying for an easy death or a life without woe. That was indeed her plan: get up at dawn, go to the temple, light the lamp at dusk without fail, offer good and bad advice to the children at right and wrong occasions, carry on like this for two or three years, then fall ill, be bedridden for four-five days or a couple of weeks, watch the kids fuss about how Amma, who was so full of beans, had become so weak, sip the sacred waters from the Ganga from all three, and finally, depart. After that, the children were to conduct the funeral ceremonies and feast in grand style and observe the death anniversary sacrifice and feast year after year. As a soul, she would hover in the air and listen to children advising grandchildren before their marriage ceremonies or housewarming functions, 'Light a lamp and pray before Ammoomma's picture, my dear.' And attain moksha, final salvation, in the end. After everything was over, acquaintances were to marvel, 'Oh, our Sreekumari saar, ... she was a blessed soul no doubt—how she died, so peaceful!' Instead of all this, to have got into this monkey business at sixty-plus—will these folks spare her? Something flared inside her. Then another kick landed on her lower belly. Again, again, unendingly. Her thigh bones began to break under the strain. Sreekumari Amma's strength failed; her courage vanished. She shrieked:

'Take me to Sumitha ... please ... I am about to give birth ...'

Son and daughter-in-law panicked seeing Amma heave and recede like waves upon the sea. The son jumped up to hold her tight. Daughter-in-law dragged a chair and tried to get her to sit down. Grandson ran to call his Uncle and Doctor Aunt. In that flurry nobody heard Sreekumari Amma say that she was about to give birth; the son thought that she meant 'give up the ghost'. Who takes notice when one utters the truth these days? As Sreekumari Amma screamed in her lost voice, Sumesh and Sumitha came. Sumitha began to examine her mother.

'Inside the room … please … only you …' Sreekumari Amma told her daughter in between her agony.

When they were inside, she told her daughter in a sinking tone: 'My dear … I won't hold back anything from you. I'm going to give birth. I've caused such shame to you at this age. Kill me with an injection, please …'

What is Amma saying, Sumitha was stunned. Sreekumari Amma writhed in pain on the bed.

'Aren't you a doctor? Look here. This is labour pain. I'm going to give birth.'

Sumitha stared in horror at the distended belly. She saw it shift as if about to give birth. Frightened, she wanted to cry out loud. But Sreekumari Amma pressed her hand hard.

'My dear, don't tell anyone this ... please, don't let Satish and Sumesh know ... Don't tell Malini ...'

Sumitha forgot that she was a doctor and the mother of two; she took fright like a little child. Sreekumari Amma begged her daughter again:

'Please tell everybody that this is your child ... Please, please bring him up yourself ... Please call him Kannan ...'

Saying this, she screamed, 'My Lord, God, Guruvayoorappaa ...' There he lay, inside her belly, upon the peepal-leaf, sucking his toe. Sreekumari Amma felt as if her bones were being pulverized. His head was coming out now. Kannan. He who had slept in his mother's womb for forty years. Here he comes with the sandal mark on his forehead, peacock feathers in his hair, flute in his hands. Sreekumari Amma's body trembled. She thrashed about on the bed. The sight of it made Sumitha feel giddy. She pumped the sedatives she had into her mother's body. Sreekumari Amma smiled and wept in her pain. Remembered Him. Then it was dark. Sumita must have injected medicines that pregnant women shouldn't have. When she woke up, the delivery was over. But her body had failed. She was paralysed.

Sumitha set up a cradle next to Amma's cot. Sreekumari rocked it and sang lullabies, lying flat on her back. The rocking cradle reminded her of Fantasy Park and Crazy Love. Probably because of the Resemblance. *Smritimaan*: Resemblance evokes memory. *Bhraanthimaan*: Resemblance evokes delusion. And finally ...

The Hanging-Cot

There was something evil about Grandma's death. She was found dead, lying on the hanging-cot that hung in the wide portico of our house. The cot rocked steadily, south to north. I went to the front of the house, rubbing my eyes, the saliva sticking to my cheeks like dried-up milk-cream. My sleep-saturated eyes saw the hanging-cot rock. A gust of wind whirled wild in the narrowness of the portico. Rows after rows of yellow leaves from the big jackfruit tree and dry mango blossoms swirled in it. The wind bore the scent of karpooradi oil. It puffed up the pleats of my small petticoat, which billowed into a white umbrella. Grandma lay upon the cot in the wind, her head pressed on her right shoulder, her long glossy black hair loose, touching the floor. Her mundu had come off her waist, threatening to leave the body. I called to her but Grandma didn't open her eyes. Only her pretty belly moved, beneath the neryathu. I placed my little hand on it. Something moved inside, like a kitten playing hide-and-seek under the sheets. I pulled my hand off and ran out.

Milking-man Prabhakaran was already in the cowshed in the east-side yard. He was rubbing butterfat on Ponni's udder. The calf with a pretty mark on its forehead nuzzled her udder hungrily. The teats filled. I waited, my saliva-stained mouth open, to see the milking-man's nimble fingers weave the first strand of milk into the silver pitcher. The cow kicked first. He called her some dirty word. Then he stroked her udder gently. Scratched her neck lovingly. Held out the pitcher at the right moment. The cow obliged. In front of our eyes, the milk turned red. Blood squirted from the teats. Prabhakaran sprang up. I have not been able to drink milk after that. Whenever I saw milk, I saw the colour of blood in it. I have not been able to love anyone after that. Whenever I warmed towards someone, something like the hanging-cot with that creak-creak sound rocked back and forth inside me. I was always afraid that if I put my hand on the bellies of people I love, I would feel something move inside, like a kitten playing hide-and-seek.

I had been mulling over these very things when they took me to the exorcist's kalam. The exorcist was a young man. He had nice eyes and soft lips. I don't like men with big thick lips. They remind you of milking-men. I liked the exorcist. But will he be as good-looking when the thelli-powder falls upon my face, and I shake furiously in my trance with my hair loose and the wild stare in my eyes? That's what I want to know.

When the exorcist streaked his hand upon the three-pronged lance, blood spurted. He made a mark on my forehead with it. I liked that too. Till now, all the exorcists I had met had used the red sindoor powder bought from the shop. Who wants that? This is what I like. Real blood. The same blood that spurted out of Ponni cow's udder. His blood was refreshingly cool. And ardent too. When it crept down towards the tip of my nose, I shut my eyes involuntarily.

'Show me your right hand.' The exorcist said. I held out my left.

'The right hand.'

His voice was still gentle. I clenched my right hand. Is he worthy of seeing this hand? Did he have the strength to bear its touch? I felt true compassion for him.

101

He closed his eyes, held the lance close to his chest, and forcibly opened my clenched right hand. I sat inside the kalam and looked at him, amused.

'This hand is of more than one woman …'

He looked up at me as if he had found out a lie.

'I can feel the touch of two women.'

Holding the lance close to his chest, he asked, 'Who is the other woman?'

I opened the hand wide. The palm with five fingers looked like a big spider. I extended my fingers and touched his beard. I touched his cheeks and bushy eyebrows. He started. I pulled my hand away.

'Who is it?' he asked again. 'Who all?' 'Not an old woman.' He said, 'Not young either.'

'Right …' I said. 'Aged forty or forty-five. A fair-skinned woman whose tresses reached well below her knees. Married at fourteen. A mother at fifteen. A widow at seventeen. A grandmother at thirty-seven.'

The exorcist called his assistants. When they were discussing the next rite, I went to my hanging-cot. As I sat on it, I saw the lake again. The old lake. Gusts of wind came up the steps and dropped down heavy upon the hanging-cot, freshly bathed in the lake, laden with wet bundles of washed clothes. The hanging-cot rocked creak-creak-creak. They pulled at the border of my white silk sari, just the same way they used to tug gaily at Grandma's neryathu with narrow patterns on its border. Grandma lay upon the cot, her face away from the door of the portico, with her right hand hanging and blood oozing from her mouth. I cried, sitting with my back to the half-wall, wearing nothing but my white petticoat. My eyes were on Grandma's belly. A terrible worry gripped me, whether that thing still moved in her belly. People stood around the portico and its steps arguing whether Grandma had a heart attack or not and whether she needed a post-mortem or not. As I sat with my eyes open, Grandma opened her eyes, still lying on the cot. Not bothering to wipe the blood that had trickled out of the corner of her mouth like saliva, she smiled at me. As I stared back unable to blink, something like a calf leaped up in her belly. They took her to be bathed in the lake. I followed them, weeping. They drew greenish water from the lake and poured it in pitchers on her body. The blood in the corner of her mouth flowed down with the water. The lake had offered water; Grandma repaid that loan with her blood. I watched, with my mouth open, the water from the lake return to it as blood. I have never been able to cry since then.

'What should we offer you to leave this body?' the youthful exorcist asked. I shook my loosened hair and laughed at him. His blood flowing down my forehead was creeping close to my lips. Maybe it will stick to my cheeks like dried-up saliva. As I was thinking of ways of returning to him the blood I had taken from him, the night-queens burst into bloom outside. This is the hour in which the heavy night winds come up from the lake. The wind will be ever so slightly moist. The leaves of the jackfruit tree fall off aroused. Scent and touch guide the little bats; they make their way through the dark and press their lips on golden mangoes. No, won't leave. Grandma won't leave. She will gently walk up here in her black-stripe-bordered mundu, her neryathu carelessly thrown over her shoulders, her red-coloured blouse, and the streak of sacred ash on her forehead. The knee-length hair will roll down her back and be tied at the tip. Grandma will come and sit on the hanging-cot. The red sindoor from the goddess's temple will shine within the sacred-ash streak like Siva's third eye. The hanging-cot slowly rocked, creak-creak. Grandma will tell me the story of Little Krishna.

They lay her on a stunningly green banana-leaf. On the head-side, they lit a brass lamp. Grandma filled the space of the leaf. A red butterfly flew in, mistaking the single wick in the coconut-shell placed just behind her head for a flower. It circled me and landed on Grandma's lips. Then it dropped down into the coconut shell. The red wings melted into the golden flame. That looked like the blood of the flame. Anyhow, nothing has ever made me sad after that.

'What should we offer you to leave this body?'

The young man who was the exorcist looked into my eyes. I gently rocked upon Grandma's hanging-cot, not paying attention to him. There was plenty of moonlight, too, the night Grandma died. The moonlight was the colour of milk. This moonlight is the milk that has been spilt from the milk-pitcher in the sky, Grandma said. The flowers of the night and the moths are so white because the milk fell on them, she had said. Who spilt the pitcher of milk? Little Krishna, Grandma said. She told me stories of mischievous Little Krishna, who broke the milk-pot in the hanging-basket, and sucked the milk from the udders of cows. I heard the tinkle of Krishna's anklets. I breathed in the scent of fresh milk.

'Tell me.'

The exorcist pulled out his cane.

'Leave this body at once.'

I looked at him laughingly. He is good, this chap. A young fellow. If his hair were combed and put up with a peacock feather, he would be Krishna, truly.

Grandma was alone on her pyre. The chopped-up branches of the mango tree were the same colour as her body. They lay her flat on it. Right before my eyes, Grandma gently turned and lay on her side. That is how she lay when she told me stories. She opened her eyes and looked at me as if to begin a story. When the fire leapt up her eyes were open. I saw her gaze through the fire; it did not burn. I lost consciousness. When I opened my eyes, terrible sights lay in wait. Grandma's gaze followed me, remained fixed on me; it had not burned or crumbled. I could never love anyone again.

'Tell me. What should we offer you to leave this body?'

The exorcist was begging now. I looked at him. He is quite nice, this chap. He should be given a flute, not this cane. Cows, and not assistants. It will be a lovely sight to see the cows shake their bells and graze on the banks of the lake. After that night's pooja, I massaged my body with karpooradi oil and bathed. When he lay down to rest after that night's pooja, I cast my spell. I drew him to the hanging-cot. The night-queens were blooming wild then. A furious wind blew. Somewhere someone spilt a pitcher of fresh milk. The moonlight-milk flowed down. The scent of fresh milk filled the air. The hanging-cot rocked creak-creak. If necessary I will retell the story of Krishna who first sucked the milk and then the blood, to the dregs. Grandma's death was unnatural. Mine will be unnatural too. I too will lie on my side on the hanging-cot rocking creak-creak, my hair loose. The blood that I owe him, too, will be on my lips, sticking to them like dried-up saliva.

Noor—Light Years of Solitude

An inevitability between two paroles—the prison. Jailbreak between two bodies—sex. Satyan thought of such things as he drove the jeep towards Kanjirappally to see Noorjahan. It was usual for such madness to take over when he crossed the jail gates at Poojapura and set out to see her. Noor was his jewel. He was on parole just to steal her. Noor was his dream. He returned to prison just to dream of her. Noor was his challenge. He set out into her to meet it. But there was the truth, above everything—Noor was his woman. It was for her that he still remained a man.

Before he met Noor, Satyan didn't know the meaning of the word 'woman'. He had grown up on the coast where fishermen's shouts and curses echoed. He thought of his father with pride. He was the local pimp, the greatest. He was even more proud of his mother. She was the local whore—again, the greatest. A made-for-each-other couple. His happiest memory of his mother was of her fishing out rupee-notes tucked away under her left breast; the fish scales sticking to them shone bright. Every evening Mother wore orangish kanakaambaram flowers, suckled the younger child, put it to sleep in the cradle, fed Satyan with rice gruel and tapioca, swept the kitchen floor clean, latched his room from the outside, fastened him to a solitude so dense that no prison could ever match it, and engaged in multiple tasks in the latch-less room on the south side. If the younger one woke up in its cradle, Father rocked it back to sleep, keeping watch on the veranda.

At the age of eight, Satyan escaped the latched room. Until he met Noor, 'woman' meant only one thing to him. A piece of flesh capable of lying flat on its back. He saw her for the first time at Nadapuram. He had been summoned there for murder. The Hindus had lost two people. Two groups set out towards Muslim houses marked for revenge. Kill the prey, destroy everything material, rape the women, set the houses on fire—take an eye for an eye. This was the mission on which Satyan set out. They were eight in the group. He was clad in black; there was a vermilion mark on his forehead and his nose and mouth were masked. They jumped over the wall into the yard of a large two-storeyed house, smashed the teak door and barged in. The screams of women and children rent the air. Satyan doesn't remember the interiors of the house. A kind of madness had taken over. For some strange reason, he was left alone in the house. Smashing everything in his way, he reached a small side room and pushed open the lightly shut door. Something shivered on the bed in the light of the bed lamp. The hunter in him sprang awake, alert. He recognized it to be a woman. A flat-on-its-back piece of flesh. She had a peculiar orangish glow—like the fish the folks on the seashore call 'unny mary'. He doesn't remember whether she screamed or begged to be spared that moment. But he does remember the noise of her nightgown tearing as he yanked at it with his left hand, the sword-stick in his right. He also remembers that the half-read book inverted on her chest fell off, that her bedpan rattled when the sword-stick hit against it as he shifted it, that he instinctively turned on the powerful lamp above her head, that his eyes, already blinded for a moment by the glare of the lamp, were further dazzled by the brilliance of her beauty. She glowed, like a ripe orange. Satyan's hands tingled. He turned his bloodthirsty eyes on her. Everything was in place—her eyes, nose, cheeks, neck, breasts, navel, belly. But below that—the searing brute in Satyan ground to a stupefied halt. No thighs followed. Instead two strings of flesh hung limp like dried-up lotus stems. She was truly a piece of flesh.

His fear exceeded hers. The sword-stick slipped out of his hands. He turned to run but came back; the reaction made him feel ashamed. The bedpan was full. He emptied it in the toilet, cleaned it and brought it back. Then draped her in another nightgown he found hanging on the clothes stand. As he walked away as fast as he could, the sword-stick grazed his foot. Bending down to retrieve it, his hand felt the book. He picked it up, not remembering that it was hers. By force of habit, he lifted up his shirt and stowed away the sword-stick close to his spine under his shirt, into his belt. He thrust the book inside his shirt in front, inside his belt. While changing in their hiding place, he read the name of the book: *One Hundred Years of Solitude*.

From that day, that moment, she ruined his sleep. In the nights that followed, Satyan's nightmares were of the shanty town, the graveyard, the seashore. He ran through the shanty town and sought refuge in a hut—there, on the bare floor, was she. As he panted and sweated among flaming pyres in the graveyard, there she was, on a pyre newly set alight. As his legs sank exhausted into the lonely stretches of sand on the seashore, there she was, like a mermaid in the sea, her waist beneath the waters. In all his dreams, she was naked. In all his dreams, she lay flat on her back and read a book. In all his dreams, the book was the same. *One Hundred Years of Solitude*.

Until he met her again, he tucked the book into his chest like the sword-stick on his back. It grazed his chest when he sat down. He wrapped it in a plastic jacket so that it would not be tattered, soaked in his sweat. After four or five months he met her again. He had just murdered a merchant in Kochi and gone off to a Cheshire Home in Thiruvananthapuram to lie low, posing as a job seeker who had a letter of recommendation from a minister. She recognized him instantly. Where is my book? She was the first to talk. He recalled her then. Satyan's body thrilled as if he were lying face down on the gravelly seashore during high tide. When he pulled the book out from his waist and handed it to her, she opened it, a light smile playing on her lips lit with their orange glow, dipped her nose in it and teased him: 'This book smells of you, now.' She inverted it on her chest for a few minutes and it stayed just the way it had rested on her when Satyan first found her. 'Now it has my scent … Do keep it on your body …' she kidded.

He felt tiny. Each man stands up on a few ego-stilts. He can't stand women who sense them. He likes women who embrace them. He adores women who shatter them. Satyan didn't know what his particular stilt was. But Noor sensed it, shattered it. He left the room without taking the book. That evening, he was arrested. In the police jeep he felt like a coward, empty. He returned after a month, on bail. The warden of the Cheshire Home recoiled in disgust as he showed him his things. Along with that bundle were a letter and a book. The same book. *One Hundred Years of Solitude.* The letter was hers. I'm leaving Cheshire Home. I'll wait every night. The half-read book will be inverted on my chest. Come for me with your shining sword-stick, breaking down the door! Yours, Noor, Noormahal, Kanjirappally.

That night, Satyan went to the beach. He lay face down on the bare sand and wept. The sea proffered hand after hand, many hundreds of them; they brimmed with longing to touch him. The sea dragged itself towards him each time along the bare shore but slipped back. It failed each time, poor leg-less sea. White-fingered waves wrote letters to him on the sand. Satyan stepped back, unable to touch its whiteness with his hands sticky with blood. But he was like any grain of sand; a tide overwhelmed him. As he willingly rolled into the sea's arms, Satyan discovered that his tears and the sea tasted the same.

114

The next morning he went to Noormahal at Kanjirappalli and saw her. He told them that he had come to return a book she had forgotten at the Cheshire Home; her stepbrother—her father's third wife's younger son—let him in. She was in a little room on the north side of the bungalow with tall minarets, on the other side of a courtyard. He noticed that the courtyard had no ceiling in that very first visit. That was their third meeting. When her nurse went to get him a cup of coffee, she stretched out her hands to him. When Satyan held the book out, she clutched at his hand and kissed it, bursting with desire. I have never touched anyone till now, I haven't kissed anyone till now, she mumbled. Me? He asked haltingly, in pain. Someone like me? What's wrong with you, are you not the first man to have burst through my door, are you not the first man to have seen my body? Are you not the first man to have cleaned my bedpan? Are you not the first man to have held my book close to his chest … ? That moment, Satyan felt he had gained something in place of his lost ego-stilt. The vanity of knowing that a leg-less woman ran after you. Terrible, indeed. Helplessness in between two egos—Love, Noor taught him. The ego-stilt in between two states of helplessness, too, is Love—Satyan grasped that.

He managed to visit once a week armed with bogus letters from the warden of the Cheshire Home and ayurvedic medicines, until his trial was over. When the lower court sentenced him to prison, they wrote to each other. Satyan thus picked up all the alphabets. He wrote to her of his sea, she wrote of her legs and of the moment he had barged into her room in the Mullah's house at Nadapuram where she was being treated for paralysis.

—Why do you lie in wait for me wherever I go? Satyan asked. Why do you pursue me, you who can't move your legs?

—I'll come to you! Let's live our love, standing on either side of the prison wall. Like in Basheer's novel.* Life—the freedom in between two walls. Faith—the wall in-between two freedoms.

—This is another Satyan, Noor. A sandman you shaped out of the wet beach-sand.

—Our love is the prison in between two bodies. Free me from my body …

—You are my goldfish. I will scoop you up in my palms. Release you into the sea of my love.

—When you are released, come to me in your black shirt and your sword-stick like you did that day. Kick the door open. I will lie waiting on my cot, the half-read book on my chest.

---

* Vaikom Muhammed Basheer's *Mathilukal* ('The Walls').

—*One Hundred Years of Solitude*. That is the book. That is truth. Life.

—When will you come? I am afraid. I feel the numbness climb to my hips. How will I have your babies, then? How will they run about the beach with vermilion on their foreheads and surma in their eyes?

—You will be safe, Noor. I'll come. You will ride on my chest into the open seas. The sharks will wait on us.

—Satya, come soon. Let's merge like waves in the sea, like the clouds above. My legs may spring to life when you touch me. My thighs may move. My body may forget its fatigue for you.

Her letters stopped after that. Night after night, he sat leaning upon the prison wall lost in thought. Their love. He trained his thoughts on her. Her eyes, like dark shells, white inside. Her lips, as pink as gills. Her glossy body, as shiny as a lobster. The brown legs. How were they to mate? How were they to mingle? Love is the awakening in between two states of paralysis. Love is the holding back in between two yearnings. Everything around him looked foolish. Jails, policemen, courts, schools, roads, shops, hospitals, medicines, clothes, bodies ... All of this was meaningless, false. There was but one truth. A Satyan, a Noor. Their intense desire to mingle—burning, 2000 degrees of heat. Noor's last note arrived. Yesterday—two whole months had gone by without a word from her. Today, at three-thirty at dawn, Satyan escaped. Hope filled him as he got together some clothes and cash from a friend, borrowed his sword-stick, rope and jeep, and set out for Kanjirappally: today, two hearts will break out of prison.

At midnight, Satyan jumped over the wall into Noormahal. He descended into the courtyard. Her door was lightly shut. There was light, inside. He entered noiselessly, shut the door firmly and turned his desiring gaze on the bed. Today we will mingle, like waves, like the clouds above. Where is my Noor? My ripe orange, my goldfish?

There was no Noor on the cot. Only a body, wasted like a dead rat-snake. Eyes like shellfish without their shells. Wrinkled dry cheeks, like dried fish. Satyan shook in fear.

'Noor … !'

He cried aloud.

The dead shellfish moved. Noor's non-existent voice called back to him.

Two thousand degrees of heat in his breast disappeared. Now it was 20,000 degrees of cold. His legs, which had dashed about wild. The penis which has broken into so many women. A numbness was creeping into them. Noor—the essence, the very truth, of Satyan's life. He stared, unbelieving. Each man needs an ego-stilt to stand on. What was Satyan's, when he was looting, killing, raping? He looked at Noor again. Her tired legs, tired thighs, tired waist, tired chest, tired face, the vibrant love in her still-lively eyes. Love as vast as the sea.

He went up close. Her eyes quivered for him like fish. He removed her blanket. Wasted lotus stems. He kissed her inside the arches of her feet. Then he kissed her legs, thighs, navel, her shrivelled breasts. She did not feel anything. Mingling—the inevitability between two bodies. His kisses filled with deep longing fell upon her eyes. The wetness between eyelashes—tears. He pressed his lips on her forehead. Love—shining purity in between two solitary selves. He pressed her to his heart. The ecstasy in between two births—death. Satyan freed her from her body.

On his way back to jail, Satyan saw clearly the ego-stilt that Noor had knocked off. Solitude. Now it had come back to him. Noor, light. Ahead of him lay solitude—unnumbered light years of solitude.

The Jugular of Memory

Her voice sounded like the creak of rusty door-hinges. On her wrinkled throat a purple vein stood erect, defiance itself. The old woman set her glasses right and, with no attempt at an introduction, asked straight: 'Kutty, do you write?'

The young woman was quiet. She continued to look at the old woman blandly. Her gaze fell on the old woman's head by chance. Half her skull was visible. But there were still a few dark strands of hair here and there.

'There was a meeting in which Vallathol* came ... that was before we got freedom ...' the old woman said.

When she uttered the word 'freedom', her false teeth came loose and jutted out pathetically.

The young woman found it revolting.

To conceal her unease, she twisted the tassels of the blue shawl she wore above her salwar suit around her fingers, tightening and releasing them.

'Freedom, in those days, ah—wasn't everyone going mad over it? Everybody burned nylon and nylex ... we wore only khaddar! I had a black-bordered sari ... it wasn't much of a fashion those days, even a sari!'

Finding it hard to look up when the old woman was shoving her false teeth back into place, the young woman turned her gaze towards the bookshelves in the room.

There were a few framed photographs on top of the shelves. A black-and-white photograph, which showed someone greeting someone else with a garland, stood out among the others with an air of authority. The rest looked like moth-eaten, mouldy, disfigured, family pictures. The second and third rows were full of notebooks.

The young woman glanced again at the old woman without thinking.

---

* Vallathol Narayana Menon. One of the leading architects of modern Malayalam poetry of the early twentieth century.

'Uncle said I should write a poem, and I wrote one.
Read it at the meeting ...

Small and fearful, we are frail,
But even in our gardens pale,
Dream-flowers bloom without fail
Fragrance flows o'er hill and dale ...'

As she uttered 'fragrance', the false teeth protruded
again.

Her hoarse voice thinned into a low grunt as she
struggled to recite the verse. As if someone was strangling
her.

'The Great Poet ...' The old woman folded her palms
together as if she were standing in deep deference before
Vallathol.

'He called me near and blessed me, putting both his
hands on this head: Saraswati is truly Saraswati ...'

The old woman caressed her head—the head on which
Vallathol's hands had left an impression. The young girl
found out to her chagrin that a few black hairs were still
left hiding under the grey ones.

The scent of a lit sandal-stick from somewhere in the
past hung about the room. A hot wind stormed into the
room and made a fuss. The small steel flask standing on
the faded tablecloth shuddered mildly. An ounce-glass

beside it fell down and rolled on the floor. Now the scent of some medicine spread around.

Despite everything, the young woman liked this room with its many scents. This is the most airy room in the house, she thought.

'I was just nine then ...' the old woman was saying, 'but not like girls these days ... I looked nearly sixteen. It was at this meeting that He saw me and ...'

She stopped abruptly. Then she pulled at a white thread that stuck out of the edge of her neryathu and carefully broke it in two.

She was wearing a mundu and neryathu with a thin red border. The threads in her white blouse had begun to come apart; maybe it was really worn.

The old woman started up as if uneasy all of a sudden. She limped slowly towards a bookshelf in the corner of the room.

She sat down on a chair near the bookshelf, picked up each book, and examined them closely.

The young woman felt that the chair was there permanently, and that the old woman sat on it often with the books.

'Not this ... the book had a red cover ...' the old woman said rather passionately, leaving a book open.

The young woman winced.

As the old woman turned the dusty pages, the young woman sneezed.

There was not a drop of sympathy in the old woman's eyes as she looked up at her.

'I too had this sometimes ...' She picked up another book and opened it.

'Wasn't that why I lost that book? This allergy made me too lazy to put all the old newspapers and the children's books in order. In the middle of all that ... this book ... somehow, somewhere ... Just seeing old paper made Him so angry. Everything had to be put away ... No dust or paper anywhere in the room ... should be swept clean always.' A sigh shivered within her. 'Who saw there would be this kind of a need in old age!'

That pierced the young woman's heart. Yes, who can foresee ...

The old woman closed the book and took the next.

'When I wrote the first story, He was in jail ... That was when all the communists were arrested if they were seen ...'

Her false teeth wobbled grotesquely at 'story'.

The young woman got up in exasperation and went up to the window. She tried to smooth the strands of her hair that had come loose in the still-blowing hot wind. The red wedding-mark of sindoor on her sweaty hair-parting from the morning stuck to her fingers. It lingered on her fingertip for a moment like a drop of blood, fell to the floor and died.

The old woman was opening the next book.

'Ramankutty's old notebook. I lit an oil lamp and wrote the story here, in this corner of the room, secretly at night, so that His Mother wouldn't know. Reading and writing used to make Her throw a fit. What use is it to the family, she would ask.'

She turned the pages slowly.

'They say it was a big fuss when He said He liked the girl who had read the poem at the meeting ... That is right, no? Songs and stories, what is the use? Like His Mother says: women should cook rice and curries and make babies ...'

She turned the pages unhurriedly.

'He gave Ramankutty that name. Let him grow up like Rama, he said. Those days I used to like the name Ravindranath. Then I thought, let it be like He wants. Why squabble? He's my son, anyway, Ramankutty or Ravindranath? So I didn't think of any name for Sreekutty. He called her Sreekumari ... I had told Ramankutty, if you have a son, call him Ravindranath. If it is a daughter, Mrinalini. Ravindranath is Tagore's name? Mrinalini is his wife's name ...'

Before the old woman could say 'Mrinalini', the young woman hurriedly turned her eyes away, to outside the room.

But she was beginning to feel somewhat close to the old woman.

'The first story was about a woman who went to jail for the freedom struggle.'

When she said 'freedom', the young woman pursed her lips and passed her tongue over her teeth secretly. Were they coming out?

The old woman opened another notebook.

'I kept it safe to read out to Him … But some days after He had come back from jail, when I told Him I had written a story… '

The young woman looked at her, anxious.

The old woman's face fell.

She quickly put the book back and took another.

'Hey, just like this one … with blue lines … I began to write after writing "Om" on the top of the page. Wrote "Sreeramajayam" above the second story. When I wrote the second story He was in Delhi, as an MP …'

She put the book back on the bookshelf.

'I wanted to see Delhi so much. But I wasn't taken there … kept on saying, "Next time, next time" … took the children and His Mother to Delhi one school vacation. His Mother asked, who'll look after the cows if

I go, who'll light the lamp on His Father's buried ashes? … Anyway, I couldn't go.'

The old woman leaned towards the young woman somewhat as if to share some deadly secret.

'That's when I wrote the second story.'

Now the young woman felt greater interest in the old woman.

'What was that?' she asked.

'A woman author … She writes stories under men's names and publishes them in newspapers and magazines … In the end when one of her stories wins a prize, people find out who she is and come to her house … when her husband gets to know, he says, Oh, I wrote that …'

The old woman grinned showing her small, pretty, false teeth. 'My, look, what fancies we crave …'

When she put back the book she held and picked up another, the young woman felt like hearing the rest of the story. She leaned on the window bars and faced the old woman.

'What about the third story?' she asked.

The old woman was about to take another notebook.

That moment Padmakshy came in through the door with the dishes.

'Grandma … oh, have you started off again? Studying for the exams?' she rattled sarcastically.

'Oh, this is taking so long? When will it get over?' she winked at the young woman as if she were a child, and set the dishes on the table.

There was rice gruel in a small deep bowl. A shallow one to drink from. Two fried pappadoms on a small plate.

'Grandma, don't you want to eat? You've to drink this up quick, have your noontime medicine and go to sleep … I'll wipe you after you wake up …'

'Stop jabbering so loud, girl …' the old woman chided. 'I can hear you.'

'OK, so that's my fault too!' The thick muscles on Padmakshy's face twitched contemptuously. She turned towards the young woman.

'Why didn't you go to the wedding, my dear?' Her tone was tinged with accusation. 'Sreemon was insisting so much, wasn't he? Won't everyone want to see the new bride?'

She didn't respond. The old woman smiled emptily.

The young woman felt curious about the rest of the story. The old woman, however, was silent.

She drank the gruel that Padmakshy poured into the shallow bowl and walked towards the washbasin.

She took the false teeth out of her mouth and popped it into the glass tumbler next to the washbasin, wiped her face and hands on the towel and came back.

She took the pill and the glass of water Padmakshy held out to her. The young woman could see the difficult descent of the pill and the water through her wrinkled throat. The pill wrestled for some time with the big purple vein. Then it disappeared, slowly. The old woman slid into bed.

The young woman was now more anxious to hear the rest of her tale.

'The old lady had an old notebook. She has been searching for it ever since she lost her memory,' Padmakshy whispered.

'She'd get up on the loft and down into the larder ... Radha chechi was at her wits' end and so in the end she stacked up Sreemon's and Meenumol's old notebooks here. That helped ... Now she sits around here turning the pages ...'

The young woman couldn't help sighing.

'Come now, my dear. Grandma will sleep. She'll be still till five in the evening.'

Padmakshy cleared the dishes and went out of the room. She stood there, not knowing what to do.

'The third story ...?' she asked again, involuntarily.

The old woman laboured to open her eyelids weighed down with sleep and made out where the young woman stood. Then, with a cruel smile, she said, 'Death, violent death.'

The young woman didn't get it.

'When you prepare the noose, it should fall, here, on this vein …' She touched the purple vein. 'One didn't know!'

The young woman's body shivered from an emotion rather like fear.

'Don't make a mistake with the vein …' the old woman reminded, her eyes closed. 'A mistake will kill the memory.'

She stopped speaking.

When Sreejit returned late at night, the young woman was standing in front of the mirror with her neck extended, looking for something.

'What are you looking for?' His voice was full of the displeasure of the Master who hadn't received due respect.

'A vein,' she broke out in cold sweat, 'the jugular of memory.'

The Saga of Krishna

He had given Krishna her name.

He had started picking and choosing names from the moment he got to know that they were going to have a baby. After twelve whole years of waiting.

'Unnikrishnan, if it is a boy,' Leela had said in advance.

'Krishna, if it is girl,' he had said.

When she was still a child, Leela used to even tie her hair up on top of her head and adorn it with peacock feathers, like Lord Kannan.

The memory of this shattered his heart like a mud-pot flung on the ground. He wanted to end his life. Then he recalled Narayanankutty's words.

'Suicide is an emotion. Like sexual desire.'

—one of the unnumbered statements he had shared, sitting on the crooked row of steps on the hilltop, on brandy and water nearly turning to ice.

'Etta, just think, isn't suicide really a desire for a kind of salvation? Doesn't the same thing happen at the height of sexual desire, during orgasm? That's what I'm saying. Suicide is a kind of sex. Or sex is a kind of suicide ...'

He remembered shaking his head approvingly at this. The cruelty of memory choked him. He relaxed somewhat in the easy chair to stifle the pain. Lying there he could see Krishna's study room. The books on the table. The open school bag on the floor, the dirty clothes that had fallen out. Dirty clothes from a journey too long.

He had met Narayanankutty at the small provision store run by Selvan the Tamilian.

'A Mashter's come from south,' he said. 'Saar looked?'

He had smiled only because he knew that Selvan hadn't yet made out the difference between 'look' and 'see' in Malayalam.

'Hey, Annachi, "look" and "see" need not go together

always,' Narayanankutty had smiled, extending his slightly balding head through the hanging tips of plastic rope-spools. 'One may not see what one is looking for. And one may not be looking for what one sees …'

'Poor old Selvan …' he had said. 'Don't bug him, Master …'

Narayanankutty emerged out of the shade of the ropes and the cloth-bags, his left hand thrust into the hip pocket of his blue-coloured pants.

'I am Narayanankutty. I teach Malayalam in the convent …'

'My daughter goes to that school. She's in the eighth standard.'

'Really? Good!' Narayanankutty laughed. 'I too have a daughter. Here am I, in this hilly place, thirsting to educate her in Ooty, and no money in my pocket!'

It was difficult not to take a liking to the fair-skinned, plumpish Narayanankutty with his broad forehead and thick moustache. They became friends in that very first meeting. That very first evening he invited Narayanankutty to his small house on top of the hill. Narayanankutty accompanied him home, walking his peculiar walk, left hand in the hip pocket, listening to him talk. The long years they had yearned for a child. The vows, the charities, the fasts, the prayers to Lord Krishna of Guruvayoor. The little one that Lord Kannan sent into their waiting arms was just a little behind others—a little slow in her mind. The Lord's mischief!

An unbearable sadness overtook him as these thoughts laid siege to his mind. Once more his eyes reached the careless pile of dirty clothes; underclothes lay exposed on it, as if there was nothing more to conceal.

On top was a yellow T-shirt which lay helplessly open, armpits revealing circles of greenish sweat. That was Krishna's favourite outfit. The black skirt which she used to wear along with it didn't seem to be in the pile. Neither did he have the courage to think about where it might be.

Krishna used to have a little frock of the same colour when she was a toddler. He remembered all her clothes. That was because buying her new clothes had been his greatest happiness, throughout. Leela's mother was no more; his mother was taking care of his sister who had just had a baby. So they had been alone. He was the one who washed the baby's soiled garments. He was Mother, not Father, when he soaked the soiled clothes in Dettol, rubbed soap on them, rinsed them well, and hung them up to dry. The pile of soiled clothes on the floor was like a challenge before his eyes; he was seized with the sudden and strange urge to scrub them clean.

In the veranda outside, a crowd had gathered. From the window of the inner courtyard, the little front yard enclosed by the ornamental wall near the row of steps and neatly laid with fine sand looked as if it had been raped. The marks of the many who had entered and exited, deep dents made by police boots. Reticulated footprints from leather sandals; unthinking blotches from rubber sandals. In between, the marks of the bare feet of those who had come in for a curious peek. Each footprint danced joyously upon the many-hooded serpent of his heart, kicking harder and harder. He was indeed failing.

'*Sarvam krishnamayam* … Krishna, everywhere …' He remembered Narayanakutty's remark on his first visit. He was looking at Leela's collection of statuettes of Lord Krishna, and the peacock-feather decorations on the wall. He remembered that when Krishna had brought him tea, he had an amazed look on his face.

'Oho, this is the Krishna of this Vrindavan!' His voice had overflowed with paternal affection that day. 'Shall I teach you a divine poem—the saga of Krishna—*Krishnagatha*—my dear?'

'Goodness, no, please …' he had said when Krishna had gone back in. 'It'll be hard if she starts breaking mud-pots or eating up butter after hearing your story … the Yashoda in this house isn't very patient.'

'Learning *Krishnagatha*,' Narayanakutty continued to entice, 'can only make you love Krishna …'

He laughed.

'Yes, yes, of course … Didn't he floor 10,008? Sporting with them in Vrindavan, at night, the raas …'

'Hey, no …' Narayanankutty turned serious. 'Vrindavan isn't just another garden. It is the very pinnacle of devotion. The raas is not simply sex. Rather, it is the actual description of the merging of the Soul and the Supreme Soul … the truth is that no one has really understood Krishna.'

He paused.

'And not just Krishna. Radha as well. Who was Radha? A real flirt … otherwise, how could a woman with a husband and children seduce an eight-year-old? I feel that Radha was a flirtatious woman who seduced the King's son for her private gain …'

'Really?' He looked on, amused, as Narayanakutty argued hotly.

'Yes … Etta, do you know what the poet Jayadeva has written in his *Ashtapadi*?' Narayanakutty started reciting the *Ashtapadi* in his resonant voice.

'Nandagopar is worshipping the Devi on the banks of the Yamuna. When the married Radha arrived there with little Krishna, he asks her, "Radha, it is getting late and it may rain too. Take him home since the worship may take longer … " *Ashtapadi* begins with the description of what Krishna and Radha did in the shade of the wayside tree and the shady bower on their way home at Nandagopar's command ...'

It was all very fresh and interesting to him; he had done literature in college. That day Narayanakutty had stayed back long and talked much. He had split with him that night near the shortcut to the lodge, after a supper of rice gruel and lentils.

He felt that carbon dioxide was choking his lungs, like painful memories. The wheeze was becoming stronger, and asthma would soon engulf him. He used to suffer from asthma whenever it became too cold. He couldn't talk, then. That made Krishna very obstinate.

'... Papa, rock baby to sleep ... me baby, put baby to sleep ...'

Even when he struggled for breath in the easy chair, he would rock her to sleep on his shoulder.

She would lie silent on his chest and ask, 'Papa, what's that sound?'

'What sound?' he would ask, wheezing.

'Like something humming ...' She would raise her head, shining bead-like eyes full of mock curiosity.

Holding her close again, he would affectionately tap her gently on the back.

'Isn't that the sound of a flute humming?'

'Who?'

'My Krishna ...' He cuddled her, 'Who's Papa's Krishna?'

She would lift her face up at that and smile—such a beaming smile, he was prepared to wheeze and wheeze, just to see it.

That memory brought tears to his eyes now.

However much he tried, he couldn't recall when Narayanakutty had begun to tutor Krishna at home. Only those pleasant evenings, on which he returned from the bank, hearing lines from *Poothappattu* and *Kochuseetha* as he climbed the steps to the house, reappeared one by one before his mind's eye.

'Narayanankutty's doing a great job,' Leela had said. 'There's nothing that he doesn't know ... The other day he was teaching her social studies also.'

His eyes shut remembering that it was gratitude that had filled Leela's voice and his mind too, that day.

Sensing that someone was at the door, he inclined his head slowly to that side. It was the police officer with a deep gash, now healed, above his brow.

'Excuse me ...' The officer's voice was filled with deep sympathy. 'It's time for the press conference. Could you ...'

His face went pale. Tears filled his eyes. 'I can't ...' he said.

The officer came up to him softly. 'But ... the child ... by herself ... that isn't right ...' he offered gentle counsel. 'Those fellows will ask all sorts of questions ... that'll affect the case ...'

He could hear the flute inside his chest. But it played so softly; only he could hear it. His chest hummed persistently as he followed the officer.

The press conference was in the drawing room. He saw that many men had taken over the sofa and the round chairs of his home. Bearded ones, bespectacled ones, those with full-sleeved shirts tucked in, those with contempt-filled eyes and mocking smiles ... He didn't know who had made Krishna sit in a chair in front of them. He sat in the chair next to her, without the strength to look at her.

'When did you go away, Krishna?' a rasping voice asked.

'On the day of the monthly test ...' he heard her murmur.

He threw a sidelong glance at her.

He could not see her face. But he could see her legs. He was distressed to see that her legs were somewhat excessively open.

He remembered an evening one and a half months back. He had returned from the bank rather late.

He could hear Narayanankutty's resonant voice as he climbed the steps.

'*Shlishyati kaamapi, chumbathi kaamapi, kaamapi ramayatham raamaam* ...'

After a moment's silence, Narayanankutty continued, 'Radha's friend tells her, "O Friend, your Krishna sports with the bevy of beautiful milkmaids. He embraces one, kisses another. He makes love with another beauty ..."'

The question that troubled him was not whether her mind, which was three or four years younger than her body, would make sense of this. Rather, he could not believe that Narayanankutty had dared to teach her the *Ashtapadi* instead of *Krishnagatha*.

It was Krishna's fair legs that met his eyes first as he reached the door of the study room. White thighs peeping out from under the short skirt.

'Enough for today, Narayanankutty ...' he had said that day. 'Please leave now.'

'What is it, Etta?' Narayanankutty was taken aback.

'No. Enough. Let's not continue the tuitions ...' his voice quivered. 'You need not come here any more.'

'Why, Papa?' Krishna sounded peeved. 'I like ... Master's class ... I want Master to teach me.'

He remembered Krishna's face. It was like that of the Lord, little Krishna stealing butter.

That memory filled him with Yashoda's anger and sorrow and love.

'Why did you go, Krishna?' a bearded reporter asked. His teeth protruded.

'That ... Papa scolded me. So I went off with Master ...'

Will the questioner understand little Kannan's helplessness? Little Kannan who was so used to butter sweetened with the sugar of indulgence. Kannan who toddled off even when Mother had tied him to the heavy pounding stone. Kannan who knocked down huge trees in his toddling walk.

His eyes fell on the newspapers upon the tea table. The ex-MLA and the minister had screamed some nonsense on the front page. He drew back his gaze, out of breath.

'What did you do in town, Krishna?' That was the cross-eyed reporter.

She didn't reply. Only squirmed a little and drew her legs further apart.

The reporters were speechless for a moment.

'It's fun in town ...' Krishna pulled her legs even more apart with some effort. 'What all things along the road! It never ends ...'

'What all did you see?' Something like a sneer rang in the voice of the person in black spectacles.

'Lots of shops. Things. Churidars, skirts, shirts. How many kinds of shirts ...' Krishna opened her legs again. He thought his pulled-out-of-shape heart would rip apart that moment. 'One day when I was in the lodge a man with a white shirt came. It was a white shirt from far. When he came close it was a blue-checked shirt.' She was talking now.

Some shirts are like that, he whispered in his heart to his slow-witted little girl. Only when you get close does the design ...

'And then?' The cross-eyed reporter leaned forward, probably fired by the desire to lap up tales of all forty-one nights.

He too had questions: What did you do, my child? Your little thighs, on which I tap to put you to sleep, your tender body, which I massaged with oil and bathed ... Bereft of even the strength to ask, Yashoda smouldered in his mind. Burned.

'OK. You saw shirts. What else?' Cross-eyes was probing still.

'Then ... undies ...' Krishna said coolly. 'How many types of briefs!'

Some people laughed. Some murmured to their neighbours. For a second he even forgot to be breathless.

'Such questions to a sick child?' He could hear the police officer ask brusquely. 'I told you. He was the Malayalam teacher in the convent. He lured her away. Apparently made two and a half lakhs in forty days. Hung himself when cornered. The body has been released after a post-mortem. The report confirms the suicide ...'

He felt a knot tighten in his heart.

Silence spread around the room for another second.

'This Narayanankutty didn't have two fingers on his left hand, did he?' the police officer asked him as if he had remembered it just then.

He couldn't answer that question. He was reluctant to say that he had always seen Narayanankutty with left hand inserted in the hip pocket.

Not making out a thing, Krishna opened her legs even more. He threw her a furious look. Those feet with their tinkling anklets were sinking once again into the bruised hood of his self-respect; he couldn't bear it any more. He spat out in exasperation: 'Put your legs close together ... can't you at least sit properly?'

He knew in his heart that the questions he wanted to ask were different. Questions to interrogate Kannan, like Yashoda's. Did you eat mud? Did you break the mud-pots of the milkmaids?

'Because it hurts, Papa?' Krishna asked mournfully. 'Didn't Master burn me because I didn't want to go with the Grandpa in the kurta …?'

He shuddered.

The father was afraid to look at his little girl's body worn out from the suicides of unnumbered men. In kurtas, in spectacles, in checked shirts.

He wanted to ask: 'With which hand did he brand you?'

With the right hand with which he held my right hand close to his chest whenever we met? Or with the left, which none of us saw?

Krishna may answer, he felt, if he asked. So he didn't.

Like Yashoda who never found the strength to see the chaos inside Kannan's mouth, he begged: 'Close your mouth, little one … for pity's sake, close your mouth …'

Alif Laila

Once upon a time, an Almighty Serial Producer ruled supreme over the realm of TV Airwaves. The Commander of a vast army of production crew, the owner of a thousand novelists, He telecast two serials at the same time through two channels. The viewer rating of these two serials was the stuff of fables. The first one was perhaps many strides ahead of the second as far as viewership was concerned. It was about ordinary folk. The second one was about the rich and the famous. They were popular and family-friendly; the people loved and enjoyed them. The gay banner of their glory unfurled endlessly across the land.

One day, the Producer had a wish. He wanted to compare the popularity of his two serials. The peon set off towards the Audience Research Bureau. But, alas! How terrible was the sight that assailed the Producer's eyes as He compared the figures! The scriptwriter of His beloved serial-of-the-seven-thirty-slot was in carnal coupling with another serial in another channel at the same time. The result? His Highness's serial had fallen in advertisers' ratings.

He had become lax about these things only recently. If things were so bad even now, what if he had been away on a campaign into the realm of Cinema or something? Blinded with rage, he decapitated the director of the serial in a single swish. And besides, directed His production executive to dispatch him without a single paisa.

Then He turned to his nine-o'-clock-slot serial. As He scrutinized the figures closely, and—alack, another shocking fact! Another carnal coupling! This time by the scriptwriter of the nine-o'-clock serial, who was secretly writing for other serials in other channels! The shock knocked His Highness to the floor!

These sorry events opened the Producer's eyes. 'Woe! My poor helpless Serials,' sighed He.

The production executive was called up and ordered to summarily dismiss the regular scriptwriters of both serials with minimum notice. After the next episode, they were to make themselves, along with their scripts, scarce. Then, the production executive was summoned to the Producer's room.

'Go; find a new scriptwriter each day ...' the Producer commanded. 'Otherwise you and I will part ways ...'

The production executive set out to fetch all the scriptwriters he could find. Each night, the Producer would meet up with a different scriptwriter. They would talk of a new script. He would ferret out the script-idea from the scriptwriter's mind. Then, he would dispatch the poor soul, now divested of creative virginity.

Three years passed in this fashion. Idea after idea ferreted out fresh night after night by the Producer from newer and newer scriptwriters infused life into his serials: the seven-thirty-slot serial climbed to 1500 episodes, and its nine-o'-clock counterpart to 1200. A pall of fear fell over the land. Viewer-subjects stayed on tenterhooks constantly; they broke into cold sweat worrying about what story would be summoned to prolong the life of the serials. The scriptwriters were uptight, too. The numbers of scriptwriters who had not yet lost their creative virginity fell drastically in the land. Some of them escaped to Mollywood and Kodambakkam with their scripts. Others began to write for other directors in other channels under other names. Yet others turned to association-building or novel-writing. At last there was no scriptwriter left in the land who had some name or fame.

This worried the production executive who had no other means of livelihood. One day, he had no scriptwriter to present to the Producer. Fearing the Producer's anger, he stayed at home, disheartened, paralysed.

Now, this production executive had two daughters. The older one was called Scheherazade. Scheherazade was a bright young woman, unrivalled in her knowledge and learning. There was no book she hadn't read, no story she didn't know, and no serial she hadn't seen. She was the owner of a late-modern TV that could show a thousand serials from all over the world. She was also in the habit of flicking through channels day and night, except when she slept.

Scheherazade saw that her father was very worried. She asked him why he was so sad. The production executive held back tears and said, gently caressing her forehead: 'My dear, our life is about to take a turn. I may lose my job. If that happens, the only wealth I possess will be your sister and you … we have a long way to go with our home loan. Liabilities from the fall in rubber and pepper prices, besides. If the Producer doesn't relent, the only way out for us is a mass suicide.'

Scheherazade was shocked. But being an intelligent girl, she inquired about the facts. Then she said: 'With God's grace, I will find a way out. Let me be the next scriptwriter. Irrespective of whether I fail or succeed, scriptwriters will be liberated …'

The production executive had to give in to Scheherazade's persistent entreaties.

Accordingly, she entered the Producer's room to apprise him of the story's thread and rolled out a full story (per the usual conventions of the scene, we may imagine that a bottle of foreign liquor, a few glasses, and an icebox may be found there). The Producer heard her out, scratching his endearingly balding head and aristocratically greying beard. But it didn't fire him up. But Scheherazade could make out what he wanted from the expression on his face.

'If you will allow me, Sir Producer,' she requested humbly, 'I will narrate another story.' Devil take the story, I want my ratings back, murmured the Producer who wasn't happy with the story, and told Scheherazade to proceed with the next one. Thus she told him another story that night too.

Here begins The Thousand and One Episodes.

Two

Scheherazade said: 'O Blessed Producer! Let me tell you the tale of a merchant of this city. Once upon a time there lived in this city a great merchant whose ships brought back riches from many countries of the world. We could name him Eapen Varghese. He had a daughter upon who he bestowed all his affection; her name was Nina. The men of this city thirsted for the sight of her shampooed hair, lips glistening with the finest lipstick, and body clad in clothes tailored closely, to perfection.'

The Producer-Sir started to sit up straight. 'Aw, what sort of story is this, eh, Scheherazade?' He puckered his lips. 'How is this new? And 75 per cent of our viewers are Hindus ... so let's not have a Christian angle. Tell me if you have another story.'

'Yes, indeed, Sir ...' Scheherazade said. 'Let's make the fellow who falls in love with Nina a Hindu. Just a name change, after all?'

The Producer thought over this again. 'There are other hitches. Who are we going to cast as Eapen Varghese? You know how little the channels give, girl ... we need a guy who'll settle for below that. So you'll have to tell the story to fit that ... Well, since you've told this far ... why don't you write, um, four episodes?'

Upon this, Scheherazade commenced her scriptwriting.

But by then, dawn had broken over the land. She said, 'It is dawn now. The episodes to come are full of tension and suspense. If Producer-Sir allows, I will narrate the rest of the tale the coming night.'

The Producer-Sir looked at her and told himself, 'Cheeky wench! I will anyway finish her. But before that, let me hear the rest of the tale …'

The Producer went off to the mega-serial shooting location; Scheherazade went home.

When the second night arrived, she went to the Producer's room and gave him four episodes to read.

'Not bad. I'll tell the director to start shooting these from tomorrow …' The Producer allowed it, though he wasn't totally happy. 'Another thing. Add more suspense to all episodes. Our viewer subjects need something to hang on to.'

Scheherazade agreed. When the third night descended, she appeared in the Producer's room with the fifth episode's storyline. The Producer, who looked tense, told her: 'We have a problem, girl … We had an old Bollywood actor as Eapen Varghese. He has got cramps in his legs … won't do more than two scenes a day … but if we don't shoot one and a half episodes a day we'll lose money. So we can't have him …'

'If that's so, let's pick another story,' Scheherazade suggested humbly.

'Aw, no,' The Producer said. 'We're through one and a half episodes. We've Eapen Varghese in those. So we can't dump him ...'

Ah, Good Lord, God Above, Scheherazade groaned in her mind, my dad's job, my family's honour, our daily bread ...

—She suddenly became practical.

'Don't worry, Sir. We'll twist the tale. Now, one fine morning, Eapen Varghese disappears.'

'Where did he go?' The Producer rolled his eyes. 'Last time we shot him, he had settled down in his office to look at his files and had ordered tea ...'

'Oh, then it's easy!' Scheherazade's face was shining. 'The guy bringing the tea finds the room empty.'

'Where did the fellow go?' The Producer was genuinely concerned now.

'That will be the suspense, right?' Scheherazade got up to leave. 'It is almost dawn now. Let's think of the next episode at night, Sir ...'

The Producer returned from the location earlier that evening and sat waiting for Scheherazade and the next episode. Sitting by himself, he pondered, really, where did he disappear, the fellow who had been sitting peaceably in his office?

Scheherazade arrived at the regular hour. She continued: 'Eapen Varghese's disappearance is a mystery.

It creates an uproar in the land. Daughter Nina Eapen Varghese prepares to take over the management of the factory orphaned by his disappearance. From now on, we will tell our story around Nina Eapen Varghese.'

'No, no, no,' The Producer shook his head. 'That's a girl with a face like cold rice-gruel. Maximum five scenes with her per month, that's the best we can have. More, and people will break their own TV sets. Not that angle ...'

'OK then. Not that angle.' The thought of her family's want made Scheherazade's words bold. 'There's uproar in the land over Eapen Varghese's disappearance. There's pressure on Nina to take over the orphaned factory. Employees force her to go to the factory. When she reaches there, a shocking sight awaits her ... a woman in the Managing Director's chair!'

'Which woman?' The Producer wanted to know.

'Dawn has come, and we didn't know,' Scheherazade got up. 'Next episode tomorrow, same time.'

The Producer sat up the next night, waiting for her. Scheherazade arrived, and narrated the story.

But, just two days later, the actress who was playing Nina Eapen Varghese eloped with the director of another serial. She declared that she was married according to the rules applicable to heavenly entertainers, the Gandharvas, and that she would henceforth act only in her husband's serials.

The last shot was of Nina Eapen Varghese sitting down to lunch. Scheherazade made the maid speak of how Nina left for college after lunch on her two-wheeler, and how it got hit by a car. She also arranged for a garlanded photograph of Nina in the next episode.

Thus Scheherazade glided from Campus Love Story to Action and to Tear-Jerker, Marital Tension and Horror Story, in that order.

Rocking back and forth between life and death, what could Scheherazade rewrite, except stories?

At your fingertips, O Guardian of the Universe, our lives—she told herself. And at my fingertips, characters from serials.

Each night, characters appeared before her, waiting to be murdered, debarred, romanced and rejected.

Three hundred and sixty-five nights passed this way. Producer-Sir was on cloud nine. Scheherazade used many-hued tales, heard and unheard, in her script. The serial's rating had broken through the roof.

'Let's ask the viewers how they would like the next episode to be. Let the majority opinion guide the story. A special gift—a kerchief—for selected entries!' Scheherazade suggested.

'Right,' the Producer agreed. 'Viewers will need it anyway!'

But viewers needed much more. A kerchief was nothing; every evening, they presented themselves before the TV exactly on time for the serial, armed with bed sheets. During commercial breaks in the half-an-hour telecast, they wandered around, despondent, in search of fresh sheets to wipe their eyes.

Scheherazade completed another 365 nights. But the Producer's enthusiasm, too, had gone up in leaps and bounds as the days passed. Why not end it now since it has gone this far, many began to ask.

But Scheherazade was unfazed. She went on till Eapen Varghese, who had fled the country, returned (following relief from leg-muscle cramps), brought into the open a secret wife and family, accepted Janardanan as his son-in-law, and Nina, stung by this, reappeared as a spook (following the return of the actress disillusioned in marriage, begging for a role). By then, another 365 days had passed.

And by that time, the serial's rating was reaching for the stratosphere. The Producer was very pleased indeed. He summoned Scheherazade and her father, the production executive, to his side and said: 'O Wise Young Woman, this serial is spellbinding indeed. You have taught me many things. You convinced me that viewers are but dolls that dance to scriptwriters' tunes. Through the thousand episodes you filled my soul with divine ambrosia! Now I am all the more enthused by production!'

The production executive entered the room in the middle of this speech with the latest rating charts. He asked the Producer, who was shedding tears of joy on seeing them: 'O Your Highness, am I allowed to keep my job? Will you dismiss me?'

His Highness the Producer burst into tears. 'Never, my friend, never.'

Delighted at this, Scheherazade gave the serial a happy ending in the next episode. And the Producer? He aired the serial first on the government channel, then on a private channel, and finally made a movie out of it, which was a thumping hit. He ordered his serial company to enclose the original script in a golden case and keep it under lock and key.

Here ends the marvellous, wise, and rare story of The Thousand and One Episodes.

Or maybe, it begins (after all, a second part can always be launched).

For the suspense scene in that yet-to-be-shot Episode Thousand and Two, we have two options:

One, the Producer, who lost his heart to Scheherazade's alluring storytelling, marries her. Before long, attracted by a sixteen-year-old who came seeking a role, Producer makes a grand announcement—'From today, Mayavinodini will breathe life into the role of my wife'—and dismisses Scheherazade.

Two, Scheherazade gets married in due time. Her husband mercilessly tortures and interrogates her over many thousand subsequent nights about the thousand nights she had spent in the presence of an infamous lecher of a Producer. She is so utterly drained that she can't narrate even a mini-story.

What will be Scheherazade's lines in those tense final scenes in which she will be de-story-ed?

That smashing dialogue, God Almighty, be so good as to write. By Your-self.

The Heart Attacks Us

Savithri Amma, Wife of Aalappaattu Vadakkel Raman Pillai Raghavan Pillai, had a single, sole, desire in life: an unfettered, unencumbered heart attack. All of it, just for herself. Soon after heart attacks became fashionable, and cool Singapore-returned moneybags began to die of them, she has been praying and praying: 'My dear Lord Sreevallabhan, why can't you give me a heart attack too?'

Well, heard about this Husband of Sree [the Goddess of Prosperity]—this Sreevallabhan? Stands six feet tall inside the sanctum sanctorum of his temple. Quite a looker. What a body—anointed with golden, fragrant sandal-paste, glowing in a gold-bordered mundu, good enough to floor any feminist! And how talented—a Kathakali enthusiast, a first-rate Sanskrit scholar. Naturally, a pucca male chauvinist. Can't stand the sight of women. Long time ago, a sweeper-woman dared to throw a longing glance at him. He cursed her then and there—and she turned into stone. Thenceforth women were not to be allowed to enter the shrine, and that was an order. They were allowed darshan only on special days. On those days he smeared himself with soot and wore a country-bumpkin's areca-skin hat. Oh, the trouble when men have too much personality and erudition! Then communism, E.M.S. Nambutiripad and socialism arrived, and he made some concessions. Even then it was, oh, women? Aww ... well, OK. Can't blame him. The wenches of Tiruvalla are famous. Self-sufficient, self-willed and brilliant at getting things done for themselves. And really smart at asking, Oh, really, was it *really* like that—once the job gets done.

But poor Savithri Amma is meek as a mouse. She has never worn a sari in her life. Never worn a brassiere; never even thought of panties! She has always been in a double mundu, neryathu and a high-necked blouse of coarse cloth. Under that, unfailingly, a bodice of even coarser cloth. She has never faced the temple's sanctum without the under-mundu tucked between her legs, the tattu. Never prayed with her folded hands above her shoulders. Never performed a salutation on her knees. Her ekadashi and pradosham fasts were of flawless perfection; her adherence to Husband [of Sree]'s likes and dislikes was nonpareil. Tiruvatira and the Monday-fast were honoured without fail. She circumambulated the sanctum according to strict conventions, reciting the sahasranaamam and the dashaavataara shlokam. Why, she even sponsored the famous paala feast. So what? Did Husband [of Sree] melt? Did He relent? Ha, he's quite a sharp one. The legend is that once his sister, who had resolved to swipe a golden seat from his temple, came to visit him with some heavy-duty gum smeared on her bums. But this one's really too smart—He had smeared the seat with coconut oil in advance so the seat didn't stick on the lady's bums! So it was only to be expected that whatever Savithri Amma saw somewhere in the corner of her mind, Husband [of Sree] would see written all over the sky. If Savithri Amma made a vow that she would bathe and pray for twelve days, He would grant her a pregnancy. No trouble for the next one and a half years—too much to do with the delivery, post-delivery and breastfeeding! In any case many of women's problems will be solved only if they are impregnated frequently enough. So she has had seven or eight by now. But that stopped after some time. Savithri Amma, too, was wiser by then, like most women. Nothing she prayed for would be given to her. Nothing she craved for would be attained. Your arms and legs will get stuck together if you toy with the adhesive of desire. Your bums will be a mess. You won't be able to sit tight on a single seat with the excuse that you got stuck on it. The owner of the seats would have smeared them generously with oil so that no gum could possibly fix you on them. For Savithri Amma, her children became her glue. She got stuck on them, they got stuck on her. Delicate webs of glue criss-crossed her. Time flew, and the webs went away, seeking other prey. Savithri Amma became alone once more. Because she had nowhere to go and no one to lean on, she once again took refuge in Sreevallabhan's shrine. Sreevallabha, I need nothing more. Just one favour. A heart attack—unencumbered, unfettered, swift.

Did Sreevallabhan relent? Did His heart melt? Whatever it was, it happened on the eve of Vishu, the day before Savithri Amma's sixtieth birthday. In that auspicious hour between eleven and eleven-thirty. That's when Raghavan Pillai has his broken-rice gruel. The boiling gruel should be unfailingly upon the table in the small steel basin covered with the steel plate with curved edges. Near it, in a small bowl, the curry of yams cooked in coconut and red-chilly paste and doused with fried mustard should be offered. The offering, however, would be complete only when sliced salted mangoes were placed upon a steel plate, along with ripe and unripe kanthari-chillies. Savithri Amma had been searching for the correct sort of salted mango as the ritual demanded. They were in an ancient Chinese urn, the height of two people. If you climb up the little ladder and dip your hand in it, you can hear the sighs of shrivelled and hardened raw mangoes soaked for long in salt-impregnated water. Oh, which old house doesn't have a Chinese urn for raw mangoes in brine? That day, when she loosened the cloth wound around the lid, she remembered how she had felt when she used to go each time into the confinement room in the southern part of the house. The piercing odour of placenta and blood. Sreevallabhan's divine and deadly discus, the Sreechakram, zoomed towards her just that moment. Something happened inside her—the tied-up mouth of the salted-mango urn inside her was first slashed open. The salted mangoes had all vanished; they had been served at her favourite God's paala feast. The brine of tears that had been left behind erupted in a flood. The salt's smouldering fire crept slowly through Savithri Amma's veins. Her feet slipped from the ladder. Her bowl fell to the floor, rolled off right up to the lower step of the veranda and made quite a party.

Savithri Amma's four children were home on vacation. It was Plus-Two student Ammu, grandchild by her sixth daughter, the Plus-Two teacher Ramakutty, who first discovered that Grandma had a fall. She screamed; Ramakutty came running, and right behind her, the seventh child now living in Ernakulam, the much-coddled Sumakutty. At her daughters' anxious queries of Oh-what-happened-Mother, Savithri Amma gushed joyfully, 'Never mind, Edi. Sreeveallabhan heard me, at last!'

In the portico Raghavan Pillai lay on his easy chair in his spotless gold-bordered dhoti and neryatu, with the sandal mark on his forehead and the golden string of rudraksha beads, each as big as a gooseberry, on his chest. He was reciting in his dignified and resounding voice a poem he used to teach seventh-standard students of Prince Marthanda Varma School:

The wild woods, where He was to dwell
Is proud Ayodhya, the Kings' Marvel
The humble hut where He is to rest,
Is her pearly palace, nevertheless.

Declaring thus, she tarried not
Fixed at heart, she hurried on
In haste to keep her solemn vows
Of chaste wifehood, and wifely love.

Chithrasala. Ulloor S. Parameswara Aiyar's famous lines set to the metre *Nathonnatha*. Because they had heard it so many times, the children didn't notice it as they were taking Mother out of the house. Raghavan Pillai, too, did not hear the procession through the front veranda and the ceremonial shouts. As the oldest son Rajendran started the car, only Savithri Amma could make out:

Woven bark, rough and coarse
Around her delicate waist she wore
Followed her Lord, ever so bold
His very shadow, through wild roads.
Fatigue she felt not, pain, she forgot,
The Chaste Consort, virtue's true resort.

In the car, Savithri Amma lay soaking in sweat on Sumakutty's lap. She felt that she was standing, drenched from the purifying ritual dip, inside Sreevallabhan's shrine. There she was, standing with her hands folded, right in front of the sanctum. The worship was over. It was time to take in the offerings. The doors of the sanctum swung shut. Women must now move away beyond polluting distance.

Savithri Amma lay beyond polluting distance, for four full days, in the ICU. On the fourth day, second son Surendran stood behind Father's easy chair and cleared his throat loudly.

'Hmm … ?'

'Amma's situation …'

'Hmm … ?'

'She has four or five blocks … The surgery is tomorrow.'

'Isn't that expensive?'

Raghavan Pillai curled his fingers around the rudraksha chain and gave it a thought.

'Anyway, let me see her.'

Meanwhile, Savithri Amma's condition was quite like the shrivelled-up tender mango floating in brine. It was rather pleasurable. She felt weightless. Ageless. Then she felt someone beside her. She shuddered. Who's this? Husband [of Sree], in person? Six feet tall. Gold-bordered mundu. Gold-bordered neryathu. Golden string of rudrakshas … her visible God! Looking at Savithri Amma who was struggling to open her eyes, he put it straight:

'Savithri, this is indeed me. I came here to tell you something. I have never ever called you tenderly by your name. Never spoken a kind word to you. We have been together since the past forty or forty-five years. At the strike of four every morning, you brought me black coffee with melted ghee to my bedside. At the strike of eight, you served piping hot, deliciously soft, flower-like idlis with sambar and hot podi. At eleven, you kept ready broken-rice gruel with yam-curry sprinkled with fried mustard and sliced salted mangoes with kanthari chillies. At three-thirty at noon, you poured out milk-coffee and served with it sweetened and softened beaten rice; you never delayed for a minute the rice gruel, the lentils and roasted poppadom for supper. At night you always had cumin-water ready in the bronze pitcher near my bed. If I got up to ease myself, you would always be up before me to switch on the lamp before I reached the toilet. If I even grunted mildly in my sleep, you asked me if I needed water or something else. You laundered my clothes, starched, and ironed them to perfection. Whether it was a pen, or an umbrella, or my glasses, you always put the things I needed where I could easily find them. In return for all this I gave you nothing but eight children. Did you have enough to eat, did you have enough clothes to wear, enough oil for your bath ... I never asked. We never chatted together. We have never visited any place as a couple.'

Savithri Amma's ECG rippled. She smiled at her husband in sheer delight and recited in her mind:

A Man's wife, in happy times
Is but a humble co-wife,
To Lakshmi, on her lotus bright
Blessed Fortune, truest Light.

But oh! In times of woe, of grief
Chaste wives may find real relief
Sheer joy, Fulfilment of their Role
Serving the Lords of their Heart and Soul.

Chithrasala, again. Ulloor S. Parameswara Iyer. Set to *Nathonnatha*. Raghavan Pillai had heard it in his heart. But he didn't show it.

'Mistakes were made. You must forgive me.'

And then? As if he had decided it beforehand, the grand and solemn gentleman even took up Savithri Amma's left hand all pierced with intravenous needles, and held it to his lips! He let out a soft sigh and gently caressed her wrinkled, work-worn palm, rough as dried-up glue. His own palm was soft, tinged with the pleasant scent of coconut oil—it had never known work.

'If there is another life, Savithri ...'

He didn't have to finish. Before that, Wham! After all, the sweet water had fallen upon dried-up mangoes that had languished in brine this long—the salted mango swelled and split apart. The oars rose and fell in the ECG; the boat ran into a sandbank and got stuck. Suffice to say that by the time the doctors and nurses hurried to her side, Savithri Amma's heart had attacked and killed her.

The funeral rites were over, and everyone went their separate ways. It was decided that Sumakutty should stay at the family home to look after Father, and that her husband Shekharan and their children should come home on weekends.

On the first of those weekends, Shekharan hurried back to see his wife. The *Chithrasala* recitation was still on in the front veranda of the Aalappaat Vatakkel homestead.

That thorns, the stones, of forest-ways
Were far tender than blossoms fair
Beneath Chaste Ladies' lotus-feet
She proved, her Lord's true help-meet.

Shekharan, who had hurried towards the kitchen eager to see his wife, was shocked.

Sumakutty, who had flitted about Ernakulam in salwars and skirts and sleeveless tops, was now in: undermundu, mundu, neryathu.

And only that? The moment she saw Shekharan, goodness knows why, she folded her palms together and:

My Lord Sreevallabha, for me too, a ... !

Coming Out

Coming Out

Death, neither male nor female. It took John too.
He was to be buried at Wood Green, the day after
New Year. There would be twenty-two mourners. That
was the first funeral Seba attended in London. She had
never witnessed such a death in her four years' experience
as a nurse.

She arrived early at Wolves Lane. The church and its
grounds were deserted. She stood behind the marble Pieta
in the bone-piercing cold, trying to keep warm, crossing
her arms on her chest below the black shawl draped
over her leather jacket. A curtain of morning mist lay

limpid, like a burial shroud or a wedding veil. Out of it came the black horse with the white blinkers and the gold-coloured hearse. Behind the carriage, arms folded in front, walked David. An invisible cross bore down heavily on his shoulders. David, with blue eyes and golden hair, was a fine-looking man. She remembered Lazar, again. Lazar, too, was a fine-looking man, with wide eyes and curly hair. He had smiled even in his coffin.

She watched the hearse draw closer. The doors of the church creaked open. The black-robed minister came out to meet the coffin at the door. As it was lifted into the porch, he prayed: Eternal God and Father, we praise you that you have made people to share life together and to reflect your glory in the world. We thank you now for John, for all that we saw of your goodness and love in his life and for all that he means to each one of us ...

Seba suddenly choked. Who is David? Who is John? Two men. Complete strangers to her. People she met only because of her impulsive decision to come out on New Year's Eve. It was her very first New Year's Eve out. At ten at night she had come out of the apartment in Tottenham Street and walked all the way to Oxford Circus. People flowed everywhere in pairs and groups. The stream flowed towards Parliament Street from where London Eye could be seen across the river. She swam with the tide, aimless. The crowd thickened after eleven-thirty. Mounted policemen directed and redirected the crowd. A row of coloured boys holding hands shoved their way through the crowd, ignoring police warnings. The crowd scattered into a stampede. Some fell and were trampled. Some screamed. She pulled herself back by a hair's breadth, unharmed but terrified. Turning back quickly, she found that all the roads back were closed. Every point from which the London Eye was visible buzzed like a hornets' nest, filled with people, male and female, jostling and pushing. Helpless, she shifted close to a group. It began to drizzle just then. She moved towards the bare tree on the roadside. Just when she was cursing the moment she had decided to come out, John called to her from behind: 'Sister, will you please do me a favour?' Fear overtook her at first glance. Sunken eyes; cheeks drained of colour. A face emptied of life. He lived only for another half an hour. Before the crowd parted after the New Year fireworks, John collapsed. He died in her arms and David's.

The service had begun. Seba was still standing behind the Pieta; she looked at David from that corner. He was holding his breath, eyes shut, lips pursed together. When his eyes opened they reflected the empty sky. He saw her. A bright spark came out of the dead eyes, like a flash of lightning. He extended his hand. His smile was desolate. She moved forward, holding out her frozen hand. Then she remembered Lazar, again. His hand used to be frozen, too, when it held hers. His body used to be cold when he held her close.

The handshake that David had given her when they met the night before was also chilly. After the photo session. That was the favour John had asked. The Big Ben will ring at twelve; could you please take a snap of us then? Please, sister. Even in the cold and the frightening rush, she had taken the cellphone without thinking twice. It was only after that she saw David holding him close. A sudden rage flared in her. Male to male. Freaks! She would have flung down the cellphone. But no. How much in love were they. The way they held each other close. The way they gazed deep into each other's eyes. The way they kissed. As she watched, mesmerized, through the viewfinder, they raised wine glasses. Then it struck twelve and the first shot boomed. Now, said John, raising his glass to David's lips. David lifted his glass to John's. Seba clicked, almost involuntarily. They clung to each other for what seemed a long, long, while. David kissed John with lips moist with red wine. John nuzzled in David's chest. David held him close as if he were a precious jewel. Seba's eyes quivered. The bell was tolling. The sparklers were blazing bright. She felt light in the head, frozen in an incredible world, in an astounding time. This is not for real. This is impossible. I don't know this world. This world, it isn't like this. Gently, the bell fell silent. David and John separated. David took the phone back and shook hands. John grazed his cheek on hers—many, many thanks, dear. This could be my last new year. AIDS will take me. Don't think we'll share another new year. Please do pray for my Davy and me?

The service went on: Forgiving God, in the face of death we discover how many things are still undone, how much might have been done otherwise. Redeem our failure. Bind up the wounds of past mistakes. Transform our guilt to active love and by your forgiveness make us whole. We pray in Jesus's name.

The cold had broken into every bone of Seba's body. Lazar had died one monsoon. The skies had wailed, distraught. The cold wind blew hard. Shaken trees revealed the pale undersides of green leaves. The mourners' procession was thin. People didn't want to come out; they came to the church in cars. Seba opened her umbrella and walked doggedly behind the carriage. She shed no tears. Only prayed that the hearse would move faster, that they would reach the church sooner, and the service would end earlier. Looked long at Lazar's face until they closed the coffin. His face was swarthy, rotting grey-black. But she felt gratified. Lazar had solved the problem he had created. After it was all over, when she returned home, came out of the wet and heavy sari, and got into her nightgown, she felt light—released from an uncomfortable bond. It had ended there. Rest in Peace, thenceforth. But now, when John's casket was being taken in, she felt—it could have been Rest in Peace, but in another way, in another way …

John's casket was an expensive one. The brass beads on its sides shone brilliantly. As it was lifted towards the door of the church, the priest announced aloud: We receive the body of our brother John with confidence in God, the giver of life, who raised the Lord Jesus from the dead …

The small crowd entered the church; so did the cold wind. It was an old church built of granite. The large arched windows were shut tight. Upon the benches which reeked strangely of fermented wine, in the last row, sat a portly coloured man and a white woman bent and worn with age, praying by themselves, eyes shut. When the lid of the coffin was removed and the priest began his sermon, Seba moved to the front. John's face was calm as he lay holding in his hands the cross that hung from his neck. The platinum ring on his left ear glinted in the dim light of the church lantern. His long hair was combed straight; it fell to his shoulders. There wasn't even a trace of a beard or moustache on his face. His narrow lips and sunken cheeks looked smooth and tender. Death had vacuum-cleaned out whatever male-ness had existed in him. David stood still, his eyes on John's face. His blue eyes were dead. She remembered how he had held John close on New Year's Eve. Maybe that is how men hold those who are dearest to them, she thought. John had leaned lovingly upon his powerful shoulders. David kissed John as if he would never have enough of it. Seba followed them as if in a dream. She had never been held so close. She had never been kissed so passionately. Honey, I'm so sorry, John had sobbed in between. His voice broke into a soft tone then. He collapsed before long. David held him closer with a cry of despair. Seba called the ambulance. They arrived at the hospital in fifteen minutes. Before the stretcher could reach the Emergency Room, John's arms and legs tightened, his eyes fell back, he died. David's anguished wail remained: Jo, no, no … don't leave me … I beg …

The minister sprinkled holy water on the coffin: Grant, Lord, that we who are baptized into the death of your Son our Saviour Jesus Christ may continually put to death our evil desires and be buried with him; and that through the grave and gate of death we may pass to our joyful resurrection; through his merits, who died and was buried and rose again for us, your Son Jesus Christ our Lord.

Seba stood still and silent, as if she had turned to stone. When Lazar died, she hadn't shed a single tear.

Jesus, she had prayed, thank you for taking him back. The last time she prayed with deep feeling was on her wedding-eve. Thank you, Jesus, for sending me Lazar. She had been weak with joy. She had wanted him so much. He was gentle, dignified, loving. She had pursued him stubbornly for two or three years until he gave in. It was she who wanted the wedding to happen without delay. She feared it wouldn't work out. You don't like, me, Lazar, she had complained. I do like you, he had murmured. But Seba, you deserve someone better. She had laughed. A man better than Lazar? She had never seen anyone like him.

The minister covered the coffin with a pall: On Mount Zion the Lord will remove the pall of sorrow hanging over all nations. He will destroy death for ever. He will wipe away the tears from every face.

A sob escaped David's throat. Seba touched his palm lightly. David held fast to her palm. They had taken John to the funeral home together. Before that, she had stayed with him until the body arrived after the post-mortem. You know something, David's voice broke as he said this, we just got married this month. We were celebrating. Gay and lesbian marriages were legalized this month … Something like a piece of rock got stuck in Seba's throat. The sorrow of a man for his lost mate. She burned, jealous. She remembered Lazar again. The first night of her marriage. The cold hands that had reached out to her. Aren't you tired? Sleep well. No, I'm not, she was greedy. Really, I am not tired at all. But I'm really tired, he yawned. I'm old, my dear, you married a weak guy. He withdrew his hand, turned over, and went to sleep. Seba lay awake all night. She ran her hand over the sleeping Lazar's shoulder. How smooth it was. Like a chick newly hatched. He finally entered her only with a lot of effort, after many days. His hands, his lips, were cold. She was mad with love. She screamed aloud for love. But he managed to do his duty, came out of her embrace, bathed, and curled off to sleep, hands between his legs like a chastised child. Seba struggled to suppress her disappointment. Touch me, her heart yelled. Talk with me, love me … She embraced him whenever she got a chance. Kissed him on the cheek. Nipped his ear. What's this, he protested, are you sex-crazy? He began to lose his temper. Yes, I'm mad, she said, mad for you. I cannot stop loving you. Lazar threw up his hands. Seba, please, be a good girl …

The minister placed the Bible on John's coffin: Lord Jesus Christ, your living and imperishable word brings us to new birth. Your eternal promises to us and to John are proclaimed in the Bible.

We met ten years back—David told her as they were returning from the funeral home. I had just decided to come out. Come out? Yes. Come out. Openly declare that I am gay. Gay—Seba whispered. Why, David? He smiled. Why not? Why am I gay? I have no answer, Seba. I couldn't love women. And Jo? Seba was jealous. Jo? We were made for each other. He came, he touched my body. My cocoon opened and I emerged, another I. I became a man. Seba, take my word. Male or female. The ultimate truth of human beings is the body. You cannot live a lie. There is pleasure to truth. He made me see that … I bowed to the truth … and Jo came. He was my mate. Fated for me. His gaze, his smile, his scent, his warmth … God, why did he leave me alone in our paradise? David wept into his palms. Our home is full of him. He cooked for me. He made me a home …

Seba remembered Lazar. She too had cooked for him. Made him a home. Made his bed. Loved him with every aching, melting, inch of her heart. Then, eight months after the wedding, one day, feeling rather ill, she had gone back home early from work. She saw them make love. The two men. Their bellows. Their accursed, forbidden pleasure … even inside the church she could feel that day's nausea.

The minister placed the cross upon the coffin: Lord Jesus Christ, for love of John and each one of us you bore our sins on the cross.

David sighed. The minister said, Now it is time for

us to share our memories of John. He was a wonderful colleague, a white man said. He was so helpful. He was a wonderful friend, a man with a thin, high-pitched voice said. I was with John and David on the day gay marriage was legalized. Theirs is an incredible love story. It is so deep, it brings tears to my eyes. A bearded man with a soft gait stepped up: They fought for love. For life. Let us pray for them. Seba remembered David's words. No, I have never betrayed Jo. Jo was married. But he thrashed about to break free, like a chained bird. I broke up a family, Seba. I was unhappy. But Jo made me brave. All men will die, Davy, he said. But all men don't live. We have to live our life. Even if the whole world opposes … We did fight. We would be jealous, too. He could be so possessive … But no one could be happier than us. Seba, in deep love there is no male or female. There is nothing but pleasure. Seba stared, her eyes vacant. Jesus, the world is toppling. She saw Lazar again. Lazar, wiping his eyes. Seba, screaming like an animal being decapitated with the slaughter-knife: Don't ever appear before my eyes, you filthy animal … Seba, please, please forgive me. You can curse me, kill me. But don't hate me. But Seba hated him. Animal. Dirty worm. Fit for the sewer. She spat on his face. Lazar stood stunned in his tears.

They were now ready to lay him to rest: I am convinced that neither death, nor life, nor angels, nor rulers, nor things present, nor things to come, nor powers, nor height, nor depth, nor anything else in creation, will be able to separate us from the love of God in Jesus Christ our Lord ...

The service ended with silent prayers. Each of them went up to the coffin and prayed silently. Seba reluctantly stretched her hand out towards John's shining dark coffin. Something rippled through her body, like electricity. They took the coffin out. As they were coming out, the cold attacked them with all its brutality. Wood Green cemetery is beautiful. Leafless maples upon the wide lawn. Endless marble slumbering-places. Seba walked behind the others, trembling.

The casket was now being lowered: Lord our God, you are the source of life. In you we live and move and have our being. Keep us in life and death in your love, and, by your grace, lead us to your kingdom, through your Son, Jesus Christ, our Lord. Amen

The minister's voice broke a little: In the Name of God, the merciful Father, we commit the body of John to the peace of the grave. You gave him life. Receive him in your peace and give him, through Jesus Christ, a joyful resurrection.

John's coffin was being lowered into his resting place. A woman in black came running up, breathless. She broke into tears before the grave, kneeling upon the grass. David's face hardened. Seba returned to the Pieta near the porch. A heavy sigh came out of her heart. Her chest felt empty. Empty of a man, perhaps. The crowd was coming out. They were all men. They came out of the cemetery, talking with their mates, holding hands, holding each other close. They walked towards their own worlds, oblivious of her presence.

The harsh wind blew harder. As she fought off the cold covering her head with her shawl and thrusting her hands in her trouser pockets, David came out too. He smiled, like Lazar—Seba, thanks for everything. She thought about Lazar's lover. Did he weep on the day Lazar died? Did he follow him even in death? The woman in black came over to them. The cold had made her face waxen. David held out his hand to her: Martha, I am so sorry … She wept, pressing her face to his chest. Till we meet again, David said, as he went out, holding Martha close. The path he walked was brilliantly lit with fallen maple leaves shining like red-veined palms of gold. The snow fell like the soft fluff inside a hatched egg. Seba stood near the Pieta watching black-clad bodies disappear into the mist. In the distance, the black melted together. In the white darkness, male and female vanished. The earth and the sky were blurred.

She walked a second time into the cemetery and stood before John's new grave. The snow had snuffed out the candles. The flowers and wreaths were soggy. The white-clad earth was desolate. Seba fell to her knees. Someone was calling aloud from the depths of the heart's lonely vault ... Lazar, Come Forth ...

Someone, neither male nor female ...

Guillotine

Guillotine

Dying, too, is political work of sorts.

    In those days in France, the final solution to revolutionary bluster was the guillotine. Don't criticize, don't ask too many questions. There's a kind of socialism even to the guillotine. It is a huge blade hung between two pillars of iron. The blusterer is made to kneel on a stool fixed on the pillars. The rope that held up the blade would be loosened. The blade … Wham! All forty kilos of it. The severed head would drop accurately into the waste bin. The body would thrash about wildly for some time. And then fall silent, finally. It was fear that accosted

Ajitha when she heard that Guru had tried to slit his wrist with a rusted blade. Fear, too, is a kind of readiness to founder. Ajitha's steps foundered as she climbed the wooden stairs of Guru's decaying old house near the old airport. The tiled roof was covered with moss; the eagles circled the nearly deserted old airport. She walked towards the blade, pliant, arms tied behind her back. It quivered, ready to fall. This was a man who had shattered her heart, years back. It wasn't easy to face him. Guru lay on an easy chair which she didn't remember from before. The room was full of dirty clothes, open bottles, and cobweb-smothered corners. His head and body had been separated, quite some time back. He greeted her in a tired and helpless voice: Welcome, welcome, Charlotte Corday. Maximilien Robespierre greets you!

Charlotte Corday had been guillotined at twenty-four. A small, frail woman, five feet one inch tall. Dimpled chin, grey eyes, blonde hair. It was summer in Paris. Under the skies that had cleared just eighteen degree Celsius, they walked her to the killer-machine, arms tied on her back. The blade fell accurately. The head was severed perfectly. But it didn't roll into the waste bin. Instead, it rolled towards Maximilien Robespierre. Thanks, Max, Charlotte whispered. Long live the Revolution. Robespierre's friend George Danton pulled up the head by the hair and slapped its cheek hard.

Charlotte's head jerked. But it turned its face fiercely towards Danton, gnashing its teeth. George, dying, too, is freedom-struggle of a certain kind. I loved Max. But he betrayed me, the Revolution and the Republic. Robespierre broke out in cold sweat. The bodiless head fixed a fierce stare on him. As they watched, the grey eyes fell shut. Robespierre took the head for himself. He set it up in the study of his rented house, on the wall near the chair. Those who entered the room started at the sight of her head. What arrogance, even without a body! The shut eyes surveyed Robespierre mercilessly. She was murdered on 17 July in 1792. The head sat on his wall for a whole year. Robespierre touched her for the very last time on 25 July the next year, when he set out for his last speech in the Committee of Public Safety. The dried-up blood in the dried-up veins of her neck were the colour of grape wine, violet laced with black. Chemical treatment had protected the youthful bloom of her cheeks and forehead. He couldn't believe that she was dead. Without opening her eyes, Charlotte smiled: Max, even love can be a kind of terror.

Ajitha's heart writhed as if it had been cleaved in two as she sat in Guru's waste-bin-like room. Such thrashing about, too, is a sort of slogan. She was thinner than when they had parted. Five feet one inch tall, curly hair, tanned complexion. Guru had bloated a bit. His face was swarthy

201

now. Only the glow of his smile remained. His eyes still went round and round behind thick glasses. His fingers opened and closed. His ochre kurta and khaddar mundu made a weird combination. Clothes, it seems, can work as a kind of explanation. Ajitha ran her eyes around the room again. This used to be their meeting place. It has changed so much now. It was a beautiful room, then. Pictures of Marx and Lenin hung on the wall; neat stacks of books reached the height of the only table in the room. On the table there were pencils and razor blades to sharpen them. Carvings graced the low-hanging ceiling. The smooth black floor was always clean and cool. In the middle of all the books was the bed. He used to lie on it waiting for her, and reclining on a soft white pillow, reading. The bed had spotless white covers. Whenever the agony of separation became unbearable and she had to rush in, she felt like a nervous fool. Her throat grew dry when she entered the gate. Sweat moistened her palms. Darkness assailed her eyes as she climbed up the rosewood staircase. When she knocked on the small door with the antique brass lock, her breath stopped. As she entered, breathing hard and soaked in sweat, he would proffer a sarcastic smile through his glasses: Ajitha, love, too, is revolt of sorts.

Love, for Charlotte, was a revolt against orphanhood. She adored Robespierre. He, too, was a love child, born before his parents' wedding. Orphaned by his mother's death, and by his father, a man who loved his wife more than his children. The children grew up in relatives' houses. Charlotte was orphaned at birth and penniless besides but adopted by a rich relative. There she read Voltaire and Plutarch. Adored Brutus. She saw a saviour in Robespierre; she waited for him. The Revolution was Charlotte's teenage romance. Standing beside her broad windowsill adorned with dolls, violet-coloured lilies and pretty little things, she dreamed of a new world. A world where everyone would have enough to eat and homes to live in. Robespierre didn't even know that such a woman existed. He was already close to Eleanor Dupleix. When, later, he was convinced of Charlotte's love, it astounded him. When she stood before him with softly moist grey eyes and quivering lips, he was jolted, immobilized. Charlotte was not the woman to fall in love with. How could he fall in love with her? The grey eyes, the blonde hair, the small, too small, body. The body is a statement of a certain kind, too.

Ajitha wrongly believed that Guru was in love with her. It wasn't easy to separate the romance and the sneer in his words. Sometimes he sneered like he romanced. Sometimes he romanced like he sneered. Talked without a break through sex. He was eloquent. His voice was so vigorously male, one could never have enough of it.

There was something in his voice and touch that made her silent and helpless. She had fallen in love listening to all his speeches, right from that first anti-eviction struggle where they had first met. He invited her to the upstairs of the house with the wooden stairs and blue-painted railings. They could see the blinking blue lights on the airport's runway from there. Guru continued to speak. The body and the mind will seek control over each other. The Revolution is inevitable. Blood will have to be spilt, for the good of the world. Elimination, too, is a kind of democratic process. Blood will be spilt in the first entry into power, like in your first intercourse.

Louis the Sixteenth wanted a humane killing-machine. Service to the Nation—murder can be that, too. The guillotine was designed by experts—a doctor, an engineer, a mechanic. Pillars four feet tall. The blade eighty-eight inches wide, weighing forty kilos. The nation celebrated when it was first displayed at the Place la Revolution. A bandit was to be the guinea pig. The King and his entourage arrived amid lusty cheers. In the bat of an eyelid, the bandit's head and body were in two. The head thrashed about and fell right into the waste bin. People cheered in delight. Oh, to die like this! The pain of fellow beings intoxicates men. Most of those who cheered that day, including the King and the Queen, were rendered in two by the very same guillotine. The death it offers is a quicker one, compared with death by other means. The nerves are denied the chance to report the loss of the body to the brain. The brain will continue to work, not knowing that it had no body. The body will yearn for the head. Death, too, may well be a state of mind, of some sort.

Guru extended his bandaged left hand to her. That's how he used to greet her earlier too. His palm would take hers. Something would happen, like a magician turning a leopard into a kitten. His touch would reduce her. When she stood near he would loom large, giant-like. Her body would reduce, reduce and be ashamed. She longed to turn back and run away, but a sort of gravity kept her down, again and again. Even now, she was afraid to take his hand. She feared that he could trigger explosions in every pore of her body, that memories would detonate everywhere upon her, through a light touch on her lips or forehead. She was too weak to lie blood-soaked and squirming in pain. She was only twenty when the anti-eviction struggle was going on. He was the intrepid revolutionary those days; the future hope of the Party. All his speeches were about Marx. There's no such thing as caste, he said. Only classes matter. The rich and the poor. The capitalist and the worker. The traditionalist and the revolutionary. Male and female. Me and you.

As he walked on briskly, tucking a book under his right arm, holding the lower edge of his mundu, she followed adoringly, engraving every word he spoke, his very voice, upon her heart. He explained the necessity of fighting for land, fields, justice, for everyone; the necessity of fighting the class enemy; the necessity of treating everything else as inessential until final victory was in sight. He spoke unendingly of Ultimate Goodness.

Maximilien Robespierre, too, had been a votary of Goodness and an orator. He was known as such in the College Louis le Grande. When Louis the Sixteenth was to visit the college soon after his coronation, Robespierre had been selected to felicitate the King. It rained heavily that day. Though Robespierre and the crowd waited for hours, the King and Queen refused to come out of their carriage. They returned to Paris, merely waving to the citizens. Insult is indeed an education of a sort. A furious Robespierre threw away his books and strode into the rain. It wasn't the frustration of not being able to wish His Majesty that had stirred him. It was the King's disregard for the people that angered him. That's because Robespierre's Republic was another place. There, subjects were sovereign and didn't bend their backs. He became a lawyer; his learning and bearing so impressed the Bishop of Arras that Robespierre became the district judge. But when he had to deliver the death sentence once, Robespierre stepped down in protest. It is easy to kill a man but impossible to breathe life back. My mission is to help people live with dignity, not to murder them lawfully; I wish to continue as a lawyer. Pressing Plato's *Republic*, safely bound between velvet book-covers close to her heart as she heard of his declaration, Charlotte broke into little tremors of admiration. He was the liberator, the saviour. Blood rushed into her cheeks when she thought of him; her heart danced to many beats. But ten years later, when she heard that the same Robespierre had sentenced Louis the Sixteenth to the guillotine, her heart was shattered. His words had been like harpoons. This is not a trial; Louis is not a prisoner. We are all politicians and representatives of the people. It is not the rights of an individual citizen that matter but national security and long-term vision. I reveal to you this painful truth—this man must die so that many hundred thousands may live …

There are times in which murder, too, is an assertion of human rights—well, after a sort.

Guru had clear political ideas. So Ajitha was stunned when Guru condemned the second phase of the anti-eviction struggle. This struggle is unnecessary, Guru had said. We have no land—Ajitha was sad. His face darkened. We will lose power if it continues. Is that what matters most? she asked. That's an old, redundant question, he said. Ajitha was uneasy. Wasn't this struggle ignited by the Party? Guru looked bored. Look here, he said, believe me, we need to change according to the times. Faith without obedience is useless. What about obedience without faith? She was angry now. Faith is a kind of guillotine. The forty kilos fell hard and fast. Her confidence split in two. It writhed. Guru was agitated because she continued in the struggle. No. You haven't seen the truth. They were in this very room. No one can know all the truth, she snapped, getting off the soft white sheet of the bed and lying upon the smooth dark floor. He moved close to her. She raised her hand and touched his beard. Hidden in the dark strands, a white one. His eyes were hard. She wanted to weep. He tried to smile and joke. Love, in a sort of way, is liberation. My heart is breaking—she whispered. Let's get married ... Guru raised his head quickly to look at her as if stunned. Then, with a detached smile, he stood up, stroked his beard. Ajitha, marriage too, is a type of guillotine.

The guillotine drank the blood of many. The King was brought to the Place la Revolution in an ordinary cart. He was tired. His attempt to flee with his family had failed. The Revolution gave him a bizarre birthday present: the head of his dear friend Arnold. Fear, too, can work well as war tactic of a certain sort. They killed him many times before his death. So he went to the guillotine as if he didn't have a head. He stared at a soldier who tried to hold him as he walked up to the killing machine. The head and body separated gratefully; the body didn't seem distressed at all. The soldiers took the King's head around for the crowd to see. The thick black blood dripped into the sand. The crowd cheered Robespierre and Danton. Jean-Paul Marat wrote paeans of praise to the Revolution following the murder of the King. Robespierre spoke of Ultimate Goodness. Terror without Goodness is destructive. Goodness without Terror is effete. Terror is Goodness, well, of a sort.

It has been a long time? Guru asked, softly. I knew that you would come up these steps again one day. But you took long. Ajitha did not reply. She tried to remember the day they broke up. The struggle was weakening. People were withdrawing: there was hunger, illness, sheer frustration. Guru hadn't seen her for months. When it became unbearable, she had set out to see him. She climbed the rosewood staircase to his room. The door was shut firmly; there were voices inside. When she knocked weakly, it took much longer than usual to open. His face was dark. I'm busy. Do come sometime later. She had looked at him stupefied. A complete stranger. There were faint marks of vermilion on his cheeks. A long dark strand of hair clung to his chest. Ajitha stood rooted to the ground. The door closed on her with a noisy thud.

The blade fell. Wham! Her heart broke in two. The two parts writhed and writhed for very, very long. Writhing, too, is a way of clinging to life.

Charlotte had pronounced three people guilty. The first of these was George Danton, Robespierre's closest comrade. The trial and murder of the King was his idea. Jean-Paul Marat—scientist first, fiery journalist later—was next. Thirdly, Robespierre, watchdog of the Revolution. A rage overcame her whenever she thought of Robespierre the Demagogue. Rage is a form of self-sacrifice, too. Her sights were on Marat, the scientist-turned-revolutionary. Marat's underground existence in the sewers had cost him dear. Hot water, alone, eased his skin disease; he immersed himself in a tub of hot water as he wrote. Marat sat writing on a board placed across his tub when Charlotte entered. Citizen, I had written to you two times for permission to meet. I had to come now without permission … she was unfazed. All right, he said, I have been unwell. What do you want? She took the scarf off her blonde head and went closer. Citizen, haven't you heard of the counter-revolutionaries in Normandy? He looked at her, surprised. She went closer still. I have the names of some traitors, which I will give to you. He saw the knife glint in her hand only then. She stabbed hard. The inside of the tub turned red. Marat's scream echoed in his house. The servants overpowered her. She surrendered. Surrendering, too, is one way of declaring victory. Charlotte's trial was brief. Robespierre and Danton attended it; Robespierre didn't have the courage to raise his eyes towards her. Mademoiselle Charlotte, why did you kill Marat? Monsieur, she smiled, I killed one so that hundreds of thousands may live. Mademoiselle, this is treason. Charlotte laughed aloud: Max, national pride, too, can be the worst of self-delusions.

Ajitha sat down, feeling weak. Guru was caressing her palm. His hand was pale upon her dark-veined palm. The night of the first anniversary of the struggle. It was after the demonstration; the thatched shelter under which they held sit-ins was attacked. There were just eight of them there. The bamboo pillars were axed; the thatch fell. A child broke its head; there were screams. Someone kicked her hard on the belly. Sharp nails dug into her body in the darkness. Her womb was hurt. It had to be removed. She lay in the general ward of the medical college for many days. It reeked of poor women. The wound was infected. Her eyes looked for a pair of feet that should have come in through the door of the ward. Two feet clad in white rubber sandals with blue straps. Someone should have gently bent down towards her, stroked her forehead and said, Ajitha, even illness is passive struggle. But that didn't happen. Guru never even asked for her. She lay waiting on the newspaper spread on the floor of

211

the hospital ward. Rejection, truly, can work out to be a death sentence of sorts.

In the end Robespierre and Danton were left in the ring. Robespierre knocked Danton out cold. He went to the guillotine with nineteen others. Danton the Giant, towering seven feet above the ground. Dragging his huge body to the killing machine, he taunted Robespierre with a smile. You'll be next. How will you survive without me? Robespierre was silent. Before he died, Danton told the soldiers, Show my head to the entire crowd. They should see it. His word was true. That was the beginning of the end for Robespierre. That terrible day. Robespierre the Demagogue rose up to answer his opponents; the crowd expected a torrent of words sharper than the guillotine. But suddenly he was hoarse. Danton's blood chokes him, his enemies shouted. They dismissed him; declared the resolution passed. Robespierre tried to escape. But Paul Barass and the National Guard flushed him out. Desperate, he shot himself in his chest; but the gun misfired. He broke his jaw. Barass sentenced him to death without trial. That was for his mistress, Josephine, who wanted to take revenge on Robespierre. He walked coolly to the guillotine. Refused to kneel and bow his head. Preferred to lie on face up. The only man who ever saw the cutting blade come down in a flash. The guard tried to support his head; the bandage on the jawbone broke. Robespierre let out a piercing cry of pain. The guards and the crowd shuddered. The blade fell and the cry was cut short. The head rolled towards the waste bin and fell right in. Indeed, even waste bins may become monuments to history.

The last time Ajitha climbed the stairs to Guru's room was ten years ago. Those days were filled with illness, struggle, failure, isolation … She had lost her land. Her mother had died. She was exhausted. The desire to live still thrashed about. There was no one she could turn to. Their relationship had been decapitated. But the heart still flailed. The severed head yearned to speak; it rolled on the ground crying aloud. He was closing the door, ready to leave for the Party Conference, in his perfectly pressed white khaddar mundu and shirt. The lights went out in his eyes when he saw her. She stood on the steps looking up at him, her hand holding the railing for support. He was eager to be rid of her. When she began to unburden herself, the back of his hand rubbed against his beard and his eyes fell upon his watch. The Party, he said. But then, our love? She asked. Love? What love? His forehead creased. Ajitha, isn't Love political work of sorts?

Charlotte's decapitated head was a valued curio those days. It was the first thing that Eleanor threw out of Robespierre's room after his death. Her decapitation had shaken him. He could never touch Eleanor again. When she got close to him, the sound of the killer-blade rang in his ears. When he tried to kiss her, Charlotte's sour blood spouted into his mouth. She sat on the wall, rolled her eyes to frighten Eleanor. Barass buried Robespierre's body and head in the public cemetery. He threw Eleanor, her sister, and brother-in-law into prison. Eleanor had been accepted as Robespierre's widow. She never remarried or came out of her mourning black. After many years, when the cemetery was rebuilt, Robespierre was shifted to the Catacombs where the remains of the victims of mass killings were stored. The head which received the guillotine in the face and the unbowed spine were thus lost among unnumbered skulls. Charlotte became a legend. She was celebrated as the Angel of the Slaughtered. Death can well be a kind of rebirth.

Ajitha can never forget the moment when she felt that Guru had rejected her finally. She stood rooted on the spot, long after he had left. Then she pushed open the door and entered the room. The first object that met her eyes was a long strand of black hair on the white bed sheet. Kneeling on the shiny black floor, Ajitha fixed her gaze on it. On the books near the end of the bed were two black hairgrips and on the floor was a piece of a broken blue bangle. She sat down listless, staring blankly at the floor, eyes brimming with tears. The cold, dark floor. The silent, impassive books. The bed with its crumpled white sheet. Death could be also an expression of love. She got up, her feet faltering. On the table she found a razor blade. Gillette. She picked up the white sheet with the black strand of hair on it, threw it away, and collapsed on the bed. Pain is also a powerful sort of war tactic. Blood, too, can be a celebration of victory ...

Charlotte's head, which Eleanor had tried to dispose of through a servant, was taken by Paul Barass. He presented it to Josephine. Later, Josephine got into a romance with Napoleon Bonaparte and married him. One of the objects she took with her to his palace was the head of Charlotte Corday. She set it up on her bedroom wall. Whenever her eyes fell on Charlotte's closed eyes, she laughed at Robespierre's fate. Revenge, also, may end up as a form of self-praise. Later, when Napoleon fell, that face remained on the palace wall. But what happened to Charlotte Corday's head after that? That was what Ajitha was trying to trace in her research on Women in the Historical Trajectories of Revolution. She had travelled extensively for many years now. The head was not found.

Guru took Ajitha's palm and put it on his forehead and ran his fingers on her wrist. Is this the vein you tried to slit? Her left wrist still bore the marks. Oh. When I came back from the Conference that day, it was your blood that I stepped on. Guru's eyes revolving inside the thick glasses looked at her. Your blood was very thick, Ajitha, it sticks to the palms of my feet even now. Ajitha listened, silent. He gave out a tired laugh. You gave me a real scare. Her suicide attempt caused quite a furore. It created trouble for him within the Party. Once back to health, she ran away, without uttering a word. A hostel for destitute women was her refuge for some time; she was lucky enough to find a sponsor and continue her education. She tried hard to forget him. But, later, when she travelled trying to locate Charlotte's head, her memories of him twitched, refusing to die. Whenever she heard of the Revolution or the guillotine, she remembered him. She smouldered. Memory, too, can be a sort of rehabilitation. Guru was trying to forget too. Sites of struggle, ideologies. Pillars of Faith shook and swayed. The blade fell intermittently. Each day, some head or the other rolled. New heads rose up in their place ... Decapitation too, is political work. A helicopter rose up from the old airport. Four crows ganged up to attack an old eagle. A feeble old wind bent over its crutch, limped up into the room and returned. Ajitha and Guru sat in the room looking at each other. What did you bring me? Guru asked her. She pulled her hand out of his palm and opened her bag. A packet of Gillette blades—why don't you shave and have a bath? Shaving, too, can be quite a political act. He smiled gently. Then naughtily pulled up the table-cloth. I have a gift for you, too. Remember this? He held out a rusted blade. This is not rust, this is blood. Yours and mine. Ajitha tried to smile. But her heart thrashed about wildly. Romance-bluster! She was angry. Ajitha, Guru smiled with the detachment of a man who had been cut in two. Time, too, is a version of the guillotine. Even bluster can be creative expression, of sorts. Ideology, too, is a species of the potato. Love too is a kind of colonialism ...

Translator's Note

K.R. Meera is undoubtedly one of the stars in the contemporary Malayalam literary scene—a writer whose range of narrative techniques have been impressive, whose stories are unabashedly critical of the status quo, who has unequivocally rejected the latest prescriptions for women's writing. No wonder, then, that there is a scramble by the dominant to claim her as one of their own. The reigning patriarchs of Malayalam literature have been keen to describe her as un-gendered or androgynous. While there have been efforts to absorb other great Malayalam women writers—notably, Madhavikutty—into dominant literary movements (which inevitably involve positions about society, politics, culture), Meera is often accorded 'honorary masculinity'.

I have been translating from Malayalam to English and back for many years now; to me, translation has been an important tool of my feminist intellectual and political work. I have noticed over the years that its utility is multifaceted. On the one hand, translation is often a version of the 'fantasy echo' to which feminists give ear. Here I'm drawing upon Joan Scott's idea, which she advances in an attempt to answer the question how and why women of different ages and social positions connect, how and why feminists often claim identity across such vast differences. She argues that feminist identity, across times, has been consolidated by recurring—'echoing'—fantasies. 'Fantasy echo', according to Scott, involves fantasy scenarios enabling collective identification, common ground for connection. As she points out about the differences in time and space, 'It was the shared *jouissance*, not the specific historical details that provided common ground.'* As far as Meera's writing is concerned, it certainly produced 'fantasy echoes' in me long before we even thought about the translation, and

---

* Joan W. Scott, 'Feminist Reverberations', *differences: A Journal of Feminist Cultural Studies* 13:3 (2001), 296.

this was certainly an important condition that enabled us to think about it. The echoes were not across time but across different spaces in Malayalee society.

On the other hand, translation, to me, is a way of freeing texts from the confines and limitations of their immediate cultural and intellectual literacy. Particularly, it is my way of assuring that women's writings in Malayalam will not be reduced to a variant or residue of the latest masculinism regnant in the Malayalam literary public. Recent sociological work argues that women's migration from Kerala is a strategy of escape from local patriarchy but one which allows them to return with far greater means to fight it. I think there is a similar utility to translation as well. Bilingualism, perhaps, is the only way to assure that the 'strategies of consecration' by which earlier women authors in Malayalam were reduced to non-political beings may be combated. The next best way would be translation. It is true that translation may well reproduce readings of authors dominant within their specific literary publics; however, there is no doubt that the literary public that a translation addresses is a different, perhaps wider, one. Therefore, as a feminist in Kerala, for me, translation is nothing short of important political work.

But my decision to translate Meera's ebullient and defiant fiction is influenced also by the fact that she has been an active participant in these battles. The history of the feminist problematic in the Malayalam literary public sphere in the twentieth century is replete with women authors' struggles to dethrone intellectualized versions of dominant male-centred social reformisms—and in that sense, the greatest women authors in Malayalam literature have been, or have aspired to be, public intellectuals, in greater or lesser degree. Since the early twentieth century, waves of masculinist literary criticism have worked as the equivalents of male-centred social reformisms within the literary public sphere. They have defined 'women's writing' and devised 'strategies of consecration' through which the oppositional charge of the writings of these women authors—notably Lalithambika Antharjanam, Madhavikutty and Sarah Joseph—was either ignored or 'tamed'. A strategy of exclusion was reserved for K. Saraswati Amma, whose writings could not be easily 'tamed'—consecrated easily—within the dominant discourse of gender in mid-twentieth century Kerala. It is no coincidence that the longer history of the feminist problematic in the Malayalee literary public sphere has remained largely invisible: the popular common sense is that it began to be elaborated in the 1980s.

The younger women who entered the literary public sphere in Malayalam in the latter half of the 1990s and later, however, have been far more wary of reformisms.

Many of them rejected what came to be set up as a sort of 'model' for feminist literary writing in Malayalam—*pennezhuthu* ('womanwriting')—as yet another move to set up a correct template of 'women's writing'. Yet it was impossible to deny the manner in which their writings dissect patriarchal power almost obsessively. Meera's writings, for instance, pull the lid off the most normalized forms of patriarchy in Kerala, sometimes cheekily, sometimes with astoundingly bitter sadness. The writings of these younger women share the strengths of Saraswati Amma's rationalistic feminism—especially her capacity for dark humour; they rewrite the yearnings for gender peace, common in the writings of earlier women authors, in significantly different directions. In other words, they are not easily assimilated into dominant gender frameworks that celebrate difference, given that they have effectively abandoned the quest for absolute feminine difference. No wonder, really, that the strategy of consecration aimed at Meera has been the extension of 'honorary masculinity'.

In a recent work of research on feminists in Kerala, one of the interviewees commented that patriarchy in the Malayalee public is difficult to pin down because it is 'so much in the air'. I think this turn of phrase is significant: there is a way in which modern patriarchy in Kerala resembles air pollution. It is so pervasive that one may not notice it unless one observes closely, and with the help of powerful tools. Meera's stories, however, capture its specificities with extraordinary precision. Here she (and some of her contemporaries) extends K. Saraswati Amma's acerbic re-vision of 'normal' and 'modernized' everyday life in families and the workplace. 'What the Souls do at Midnight', 'Finally, *Sasandeham*', 'The Heart Attacks Us', 'The Scent of News', 'A Cat, Utterly Personal', 'Alif Laila', 'The Hanging-Cot' and 'The Jugular of Memory' trace the varied contours of such subtle, insidious forms of control. However, Meera goes further to force the feminist problematic to confront much of what it excludes. For example, her rearticulation of the theme of heterosexual love (for example, in 'The Yellow of Longing', 'Noor' or 'Guillotine' (and more powerfully, in her novel *Nethronmeelanam*) rejects the familiar framework of sexual complementarity which earlier authors like Antharjanam and Madhavikutty sought to snatch away from masculinist reformisms. Heterosexual love, in Meera's writings, is between women and men who are marginal to dominant gendered social institutions, or victims of these—figures of failure who lean upon each other. In 'Coming Out', the heterosexual woman encounters, and comes to terms with, gay love; in 'Same-Sex Sorrows', it is the heterosexual man whose firmest beliefs are shaken. At the same time, the significant continuity between the present and earlier generation of women writers of fiction is their aspiration to be public intellectuals who speak for women: their readiness to comment upon contemporary issues through their fiction. 'Ave Maria' reminds readers of gendered forms of suffering in the history of the communist movement in Kerala, which may not be remedied through conventional renderings of social justice; 'The Saga of Krishna' refers directly to the series of 'sex-racket' cases around which feminists fought pitched battles with enterenched politicians in recent times in Kerala, in which young girls who were victims of serial rape were further victimized by the sensation-hungry media.

A word about my translations: they are hardly 'faithful' in the conventional sense. They are, rather, the result of careful consideration of the different senses of meaning and complex layers of narrative that Meera's writing holds, and of the effort to convey the unique rhetorical texture of each of her texts. For instance, conventional translation may not do justice to Meera's use of the word *ahantha* in 'Noor' while the most common meaning of the word is 'ego' or 'arrogance', her use of it conveys subtler shades, which necessitated another coinage, 'ego-stilts'. The best parts of the work of translating these texts were our long conversations on the subtleties of meaning and usage. The boundaries of our creative selves relaxed with such ease and grace on each of these occasions, such that the connection we made could not be simply called friendship—it needs a new name.